Also by the Author

The Great Good Thing
Into the Labyrinth

Sky

A NOVEL IN THREE SETS AND AN ENCORE

BY

Roderick Townley

A RICHARD JACKSON BOOK
ATHENEUM BOOKS FOR YOUNG READERS
New York London Toronto Sydney

In memory of Lennie Tristano,
a different pianist,
and
for John Weisman,
a different drummer

Atheneum Books for Young Readers
An imprint of Simon & Schuster Children's Publishing Division
1230 Avenue of the Americas
New York, New York 10020

Book design by O'Lanso Gabbidon
The text for this book is set in Garamond 3.
Manufactured in the United States of America
First Edition
10 9 8 7 6 5 4 3 2 1
Library of Congress Cataloging-in-Publication Data
Townley, Roderick.
Sky : a novel in 3 sets and an encore / by Roderick Townley.—1st ed.
p.   cm.
"A Richard Jackson Book."
Summary: In New York City in 1959, fifteen-year-old Alec Schuyler, at odds with his widowed father over his love of music, finds a mentor and friend in a blind, black jazz musician.
ISBN 0-689-85712-8
[1. Musicians—Fiction. 2. Jazz—Fiction. 3. Fathers and sons—Fiction.
4. High schools—Fiction. 5. African Americans—Fiction. 6. Blind—Fiction.
7. New York (N.Y.)—History—20th century—Fiction.] I. Title.
PZ7.T64965Sk 2004
[Fic]—dc22
2003011354

CONTENTS

Moanin'

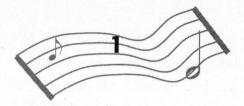

Every school has them. The invisibles. Not liked, not disliked. How can you dislike what isn't there? It's a clue when you're standing in the lunch line trying to decide about a tuna sandwich and a girl runs right into you, spilling a glob of chocolate pudding on your shirt. This actually happened.

"What were you *doing* there?" she yelled, like he'd jumped out at her from behind a bush.

"Um . . ."

The place busted up laughing. You'd think they'd be laughing at *her*, but he was such an easy target. From the jocks' table came whistles and applause. Sky's face reddened, and you could see the beads of sweat at the base of his dirty blond crew cut.

You wouldn't think life could get worse than that. Except Alec Schuyler had another problem, as bad as being invisible. He was inaudible.

Hard to say how it started. He just started talking less and less. His grandmother had always accused him of mumbling, but it was well known that she was hard of hearing. In the past couple of years, though, teachers were saying it too, and then school friends. In Truscott's class he didn't speak at all.

Truscott was teaching Shakespeare this semester. Alec Schuyler hated Shakespeare. Who could blame him? You'd hate anything Truscott taught you. Lucky his best friends in the world—all right, his only friends, just about—Max and Suze, were in the same English section.

"Well, class, who can tell me the significance of Hamlet's last words?" Mark Truscott, handsome and erect, clasped his hands behind his back and rose onto his toes and down again, his brown wing tips gleaming.

"Uh-uh!" he said, holding up a warning finger. "No peeking!"

Half the students, including Sky, immediately stopped riffling through the play.

"Well, what *are* Hamlet's last words? Let's start with that. Mr. Schuyler, will you help us out?"

Sky's stomach churned.

"Do we need a hint? It starts, 'The rest is . . .'" He opened his blue eyes wide, ready to receive. "'The rest is . . .'?"

Max's hand shot up. "History?"

"The rest is history? Nice try, Mr. Rosen, but no, the rest is not history. And please refrain from answering until you're called on." He turned back to Sky. "The rest, Mr. Schuyler?"

Sky looked like he was choking.

"Darkness?" Suze called out without even raising her hand.

Truscott turned his undeceivable blue eyes on her, like a lighthouse catching a small boat in its beam. He smiled.

"Darkness. Very interesting, Miss Matheson. Not your answer, but the fact that you felt compelled to rescue your classmate. But you see, he doesn't need rescuing. The answer is on the tip of his tongue, is it not, Mr. Schuyler?"

"Ah . . ."

"I see it there, about to take flight."

Gertrude Somerville tittered nervously, then blushed pink when Truscott looked at her. Steve Glass gave a snuffling smirk.

"The rest, Mr. Schuyler?" persisted Truscott.

Sky opened his mouth, but no sound came out.

"Exactly!" Truscott exclaimed.

The students looked confused.

"Silence!" crowed Truscott. "'The rest is silence.' Thank you, Mr. Schuyler! I was sure we could depend on you for silence."

General laughter erupted. Sky grabbed his books and bolted from class.

"'See, it stalks away!'" cried Truscott. "'Stay! Speak, speak! I charge thee, speak!'" He chuckled at the boy's retreating form. "And which character said *that*? Class?"

Max Rosen didn't even take his books. He just hurried after his friend.

"I wouldn't leave, Mr. Rosen, if you care about your grade."

"Screw my grade, Mr. Truscott," declared Max in a loud voice. A girl near the back let out a gasp as Max banged the door behind him.

Mr. Truscott seemed unperturbed. "You know the way to the principal's office," he called after him almost gaily. He shook his head. "This play certainly arouses strong emotions. Shall we go on? Miss Matheson, I'd like to see you after class."

Quite a morning.

Max found Sky in the courtyard outside the building that housed the art department and, on the second floor, the library. All the buildings of Harmon Prep looked the same, four connected piles of brick on New York's Upper West Side. Two of the buildings were on one street, the other two on the next. Between them, they surrounded enough space for a jungle gym, a basketball court, and a flower-bordered courtyard. You could pass the place on the street and not realize it was a school at all. The sisters Harmon started it way back in 1927, when this was a nicer area, as opposed to what you have to go through now just to get to the bus stop.

They kept it going through the thin of the Great Depression and the thick of World War II, until now, in 1959, it had a citywide reputation. Max was there on a full scholarship; but Sky's dad, without his wife's expensive cancer to support, saw his income rebound in the two years he'd been a widower, and he had to pay the whole tuition. Not without grumbling.

Sky was sitting on a small white bench and staring at the scuffed toes of his loafers. He held a skinny paperback in his lap, a finger holding his place. Max had lent him the book last week. Shakespeare it wasn't.

"Hey," said Max.

Sky nodded.

Max sat down, joining his friend's silence. "Truscott's a bastard," he said.

Sky gave his friend a sharp look. "Say, what are you doing here?" His voice was soft to the point of a mumble, but Max was used to that. "The bell didn't ring."

"That's true."

"I wouldn't mess around with Truscott."

Max gave a bored shake of his head. "Not to worry. What do you think of our boy Larry?"

Sky opened the paperback to the poem he'd been reading.

His friend looked over and nodded. "'Christ climbed down from His bare Tree this year,'" he read in a loud voice, "'and ran away to where there were no rootless Christmas trees . . .'"

"Shh. Are you crazy?"

"'. . . hung with candycanes and breakable stars.'"

Sky snapped the book shut, but Max went right on. "'Christ climbed down from His bare Tree this year and ran . . .'"

"Max!" Sky shouted in a whisper.

"'. . . and ran away to where there were no gilded Christmas trees and no tinsel Christmas trees and no tinfoil Christmas trees . . .'"

He knew the thing—a good hunk of it—by heart. Sky had never heard of Lawrence Ferlinghetti or this new book of his, but Max was already memorizing it. He was far and away the smartest kid Sky knew. Well, maybe Suze.

"'. . . and no Truscott Christmas trees . . .'"

"Cut it out, you're going to get us in trouble."

"This is true. Unfortunately, we're already in trouble. There goes the bell."

"So?"

"We can eat. Let's beat the rush."

Max and Sky hurried inside just as kids began pouring into the courtyard. To get to the cafeteria, they had to run up one set of stairs, cross a creaking hall into the next building, then thunder down two narrow flights into what, back in the 1920s, had been the servants' quarters. It was a crazy design for a school, but at least you got to work up an appetite. A long steel counter extended along one side of the room. Behind the steamed glass, ladle in hand, stood Big Meg, with her helper, a gray-haired lady whose name nobody knew.

"Whatcha got today, beautiful?" Max sang out in a cheery tone that grown-ups seemed to find charming, though Sky could never figure out why. It took a lot of—he didn't know what. Phoniness, he was tempted to say, but revised it to chutzpah. Max certainly had chutzpah. What Sky's mother used to call "nerve."

"Creamed chicken," said Meg, "but we're not ready."

Kids were forming in a rowdy line. John Wunsch started pounding on Max's back, for no better reason than that Max was in front of him.

No one pounded, or would think of pounding, on Sky's back.

"You gonna give us some extra today, Meg?" said Max.

"Sure, I give extra." Finally, she gave the nod, and the masses surged forward, wedging themselves through the doorway and banging scarred silverware onto plastic trays. The noise quickly rose to an impossible level, although most kids hadn't even made it into the room. Max and Sky watched as Meg troweled creamed chicken onto biscuits. They grabbed dishes of sad-looking tapioca and cartons of milk and steered their way to a back table by the window, where they held a spot for Suze. It was late September, one of those overwarm Indian summer days you sometimes get in the city. A rectangle of sunlight lay like a glowing place mat in the middle of the table.

"They oughta get air-conditioning in here," said Max.

"What?"

"Sure. Lots of people are getting it in their houses now. It's not just movie theaters."

"I know that." Sky had seen them himself. The first time was a couple of years ago in a rich guy's apartment on Park, puffing out a feeble stream of cool air while it groaned and sweated and took up half the window.

The friends dug into their lukewarm lunch. No sign of Suze.

"Hey, Jabbers!" called Steve Glass, school soccer hero, from the table across the way. He grinned at his jock friends. "Guess you told Truscott a thing or two."

"Yuk, yuk," Max called back on Sky's behalf.

Sky stared at the patch of sunlight in the middle of the table. Max did a little drumroll with his index fingers. He was always practicing his paradiddles.

"We playing this weekend?" Sky murmured.

"Think so. There's a senior party at Keller Prep. Suze is supposed to get us a sax."

"What do we need a sax for?"

"It's a hop."

Sky nodded. Their little trio was fine for "cocktail music," but for a dance crowd you needed a horn. Good as Sky was at the piano, his fingers would be sausage by the end of the night.

"We got Larry for bass?" Larry Gar was a Harmon senior, but musically, he was the junior member of their group. No genius, but dependable. Gar was one of the tallest kids in school, with an Adam's apple you would notice from across the street.

"Yeah," said Max, "Larry's cool for Friday."

Finally, there came Susan, easing her way through the crowd. It was hard to miss "Da Suze." She was the one who was always slightly out of breath, whose eyes were a little brighter than other people's, as if she were on to something and *had* to tell you about it. She'd always been like that, but there was a change lately. Over the summer she'd suddenly come into focus. Not everybody does, Sky realized. There were girls you'd bet would be really beautiful in a few years, but some feature or other never jelled. Or their smile, which had been maddeningly cute in eighth grade, began to turn hard, like they were trying to decide how to invest it, and you wondered why you'd been staring at the back of their heads all those months in homeroom.

Not Suze. Her cheeks had taken on definition, and the edges of her eyes did a crinkly thing when she smiled that they'd never done before, as if every thought she had was more complex now. Her black hair was shinier and cascaded over her shoulders. She'd also grown several inches in several directions, all of them good. Not that you could tell in the bulky sweaters she wore, and the pleated, below-the-knee skirts.

She thumped her Latin and geometry books on the table.

"Where you been?" said Max.

"Around."

He nodded at her fuzzy blue pullover. "Aren't you hot in that thing?"

"Dying."

"Take it off, why don't you."

Her eyes did that crinkly thing. "I don't want to cause a riot."

Sky had no part in this exchange, but he blushed so hard a vein in his forehead pulsed.

"I mean," said Max, "you have a shirt under that, right?"

"That's for me to know," replied Suze.

"Say, wasn't Truscott a swine?"

"I guess."

"You guess? Were you there?"

"I was there longer than you were."

Sky looked at her with interest. Well, he always looked at her with interest. This time it struck him there was something she wasn't saying. "Um," he began, and cleared his throat. "So what happened, after, you know, we left?"

"Nothing. He seemed to get over whatever was biting him."

"He was the one doing the biting," said Max.

"Well, he was all right after that."

"Schmuck."

Suze looked at Max head-on. "I know you feel that way, but Truscott's really very smart."

"All right. Smart schmuck. Bet you can't say that five times."

"Max . . ."

"Smartschmucksmartschmucksmartschmucksmart-schmucksmartschmuck."

She looked down. "I'm not saying he wasn't awful to Sky. I don't know why he does that. It's like something comes over him."

"The imp of the perverse," said Max.

"What?"

"Poe."

"Anyway, he can actually be nice sometimes."

They were both looking at her. Was she *blushing*?

"Okay," she said.

"Spill," said Max.

Suze bit her underlip, then shook her mane of dark hair until it completely covered her face.

"Come out of there," said Max. "Tell us."

"You'll laugh." Suze's voice came from behind the curtain of hair.

"We're laughing already."

She swept her hair back with her fingers. "He thinks I can write."

"Of course you can write," said Max. "You're the lousy class genius."

"No, he wants me to be the editor of the *Harmon Review*."

"Jeez!" said Sky.

"But you're only a sophomore," said Max.

"I know."

They had to let this sink in.

"Is *that* why you think he's such a great guy?" said Max suddenly.

"I didn't say he was a great guy."

"You said he was nice."

"Well, he was, to *me*!"

The table was silent. It was the only pocket of silence in the whole crashing, brain-jolting room.

"Hey, guys," Sky began, but nobody heard him.

"I guess," Max said, "we shouldn't be too rough on Da Suze. She's going to have enough trouble with everybody else in this idiot school."

"What do you mean?" she said.

"A lot of people aren't going to be happy about this editor thing."

She nodded.

"Seniors, because they're not the editor, and sophomores, because you are."

"They're already jealous of her," Sky put in.

"This is true. Damage is done," said Max.

Sky looked at her sitting there beside him, an armful of overwarm girl. He started to say something, but there was a surge of voices at the next table.

"So, Suze," said Max. He cracked his knuckles loudly. "Tell us about the gig."

"We're set," she said. "I got Johnny Moone on sax."

"Can we afford him?"

"The place is giving us a hundred. Best I could do."

"That's twenty-five each. Minus your cut as the manager."

"Except Moone wants fifty."

"Fifty dollars!"

"He says he's got a name now. He won't work for less than fifty."

The boys looked at each other, each doing the math.

"Forget it," said Max.

Sky held up his hand. They looked at him. "Forty," he said. "Otherwise, it'll be a real long night for me."

"I'll try," said Suze.

"You can do it," said Max.

"I'll *try*."

"When you talk to him," said Max, grinning, "just take off your sweater."

For a slim girl, Suze Matheson could punch your arm pretty hard.

Moone turned out to be a good investment, as Sky knew he would. With his madman baritone sax farting out "Rock Around the Clock" and other Bill Haley hits, he had the whole roomful of kids, even some of the teachers, jitterbugging in a frenzy. Larry Gar, thumping away on his double bass, struggled mightily to keep up. Then Moone swooned into a syrupy version of "Love Letters in the Sand," and the dancers clung to each other as if stuck together with sweat.

The tall French windows were propped open to catch some cool air, but the air wasn't moving. Sky didn't mind. He was having a good time. It wasn't his kind of music—he was into cool jazz, not hot rock-'n'-roll—but it was fun backing up Moone and trading riffs with him. Sometimes they'd get a three-way thing going, with Sky taking an eight-bar solo, then Moone leaping in with his shouting horn, and finally Max taking his frantic eight on drums. If things were going really well and the piece wasn't too hard, somebody would nod at Larry and he'd take a solo too. The first set ended in whoops and cheers.

During the break Sky sat on the window ledge, looking down on Seventy-ninth Street. He'd taken off his tuxedo jacket and was holding the front of his ruffled shirt away from him, wiggling it to get the sweat to dry. A drop of perspiration slid down his bony chest.

He watched Suze Matheson making her way toward him.

"Hey," she said.

"Hey."

"What a zoo, huh?" She didn't have to be here. Her job was booking the gig, and she'd done that long ago; but she told the guys she'd come to give moral support. It didn't say much about her social life. It wasn't like she was looking for action with the Keller seniors. She did dance, briefly, with one Kellerite, but begged off when the music turned slow. She didn't mind the attention, though, of which she got a lot. Her eyes seemed amused, and her hair was swept to the side and back and held with a comb, revealing her slim neck with its tiny beauty mark.

"You sound good, Sky. You've been getting better."

"Got a cig?" It was Max, poking his head over Suze's shoulder.

Sky shook out an Alpine.

"Man oh man oh menthol!" said Max. "You like these things?"

"So smoke your own," said Sky.

"Why don't you guys admit that you hate smoking?" said Suze.

Max shook his head. "You'll never get us to admit that."

What they liked was the look. Max favored Players, because they were English and expensive and might conceivably impress someone—a girl, for instance.

"What do you want to do in the second set?" said Max.

"'Moanin''?" said Sky.

"That's jazz. They don't want jazz. Look at them. Next thing you know, they're going to ask for a goddam Bunny Hop. Gimme another one of those coffin nails for later."

Sky shook out an Alpine for him, then wandered back to the upright and opened his battered old fake book to the section on pop songs. Fake books weren't exactly legal, but everyone used them. They laid out the melody lines of maybe five hundred tunes and labeled the chord changes for you. Problem was, most of the songs were ancient.

Like this piano, he thought, looking at the cigarette-scarred wreck. The action was as sluggish as driving a truck through sand. His piano at home played better than this. But there was one good thing: Here he could sit down and play as loud as he wanted without worrying about bothering anyone.

His father anyone.

"Ya know how to play 'Tammy'?" A girl came up, her taffeta making a swishing sound. She looked down as she spoke, as if she were shy; but in Sky's experience girls with blond hair swooping around like a TV ad and a tan left over from summer were not shy. He figured the big guy behind her in the checkered jacket was her date.

"Sure," he said, trying not to stare at her shoulders. Her dress was pretty low cut. "First chance."

She gave him a wink and turned away.

Standing by the keyboard, he absentmindedly reached down his right hand and noodled out the first few measures of "Moanin'," where it switches over to D major, then right away back to D minor. It was so neat the way it did that.

"Go on." Johnny Moone was strapping on his baritone. "Can you drop it down to B-flat?"

Sky nodded toward the milling crowd. "Girl just asked to hear 'Tammy.'"

"She won't know the diff."

Sky slid onto the bench and rolled into "Moanin'," the Bobby Timmons tune he'd learned from listening to the record about a thousand times. He saw Max hurry over to the drums and Larry pick up the bass. They got there just in time for the bridge, when Moone took over the lead and landed on the downbeat with a cymbal crash from Max. Everybody's head turned. Debbie Reynolds it wasn't, but the band played it hard, with a low-down beat, and couples started drifting out onto the floor. They didn't know how to dance to it. Some kids were doing a lindy while others were attempting a sort of speeded-up fox-trot. Suze came over and stood by the piano, watching. The song ended with a rumbling piano chord and a roll on Max's snares followed by a cymbal crash and scattered applause.

"What else you got, Junior?" Moone had a great look on his face, his usual boredom wiped away by the fresh sounds they'd made.

"You know 'Regeneration'?"

The sax man looked up at the balloon-decked ceiling. "You can't play 'Regeneration.' Nobody can play that except Olmedo himself."

"You're right," said Sky, but he started a fast, descending bass line anyway, then laid the 5/4 melody line on top of it. Learning to put five beats in the right hand over a four-beat tempo in the left was something Sky had been working on for weeks, listening over and over again to Art Olmedo's amazing record. He still goofed up, but he was getting there.

Moone started nodding his head, and then, at the bridge, he jumped in with his baritone, and soon they were in a sort of wrestling match, trading eight-bar solos back and forth. Max gave a shout as he came out of a press roll and hit the cymbals running. Larry was clearly lost, missed some changes and dropped to halftime on his bass. It hardly mattered. It was an exhilarating business to be in the midst of, but it probably sounded more like a car crash to those who weren't in the know.

They were just winding up when Sky felt something cold and wet on his hands.

"Jeez!" Sky yanked his hands away, leaving Max's sizzle cymbal and Larry's bass to carry on. Some ass was pouring a Coke all over the keyboard! Moone had stopped playing and was stepping around the side of the piano to grab the guy by his checkered lapel.

The cymbals stopped, and then the bass dribbled away and quit. No one had been dancing. "My girl asked you to play something," the guy with the drink was saying. This was a big person, Sky noticed, maybe four inches taller than Johnny, but Moone's eyes were flashing. He'd just been ripped out of a piece of music that had demanded his best, and he looked dangerous.

"What are you *mouthing* about?" he growled, his heavy instrument swaying from its strap.

"My *girl*," the guy said. He yanked Moone's hands away and took a step back, his fists bunching. "She asked that jerkball to play 'Tammy.'"

Moone moved up till he was in the guy's face. "So

you pour your goddam drink all over the piano?"

"Got your attention, didn't I?"

"Hey, hey!" came a woman's voice. Sky was amazed to see it was Suze. "It's just a song, guys. They'll get to it next. Right, Sky?"

"Who asked her?" growled the guy in the jacket.

"Easy," said Suze.

"Buzz off, little girl." He pushed her roughly.

"All right!" yelled Moone, and gave the guy a shove that sent him, off balance, against his girlfriend. She cried out as both of them went sprawling.

The room *really* got quiet then. You could hear Max cracking his knuckles.

The big guy got up slowly, or maybe it was that Sky was playing the scene in slow motion in his head. He had plenty of time to notice that the kid had no neck and that the checked jacket was tight around his shoulders. Tight around the arms, too.

Moone didn't wait. He snapped out his fist and caught No-Neck on the cheekbone. Blood from the kid's nose started working down his face.

His eyes widened, as if a teacher had asked him a hard question. Then fury took over, and the film in Sky's head speeded up. He heard a man's voice calling, "Boys! Cut it out!" just as the guy charged, his fist hurtling at Moone's head.

Faster than thought, Moone raised his heavy

sax, and it was into that large metal object that the fist landed, the force of the blow knocking Moone back against the piano. Again, No-Neck's eyes went wide, this time with significant pain, blood sprouting between his knuckles.

"Ah, ah . . ."

"You dented my axe!" shouted Moone.

By then a teacher had planted himself between them. "Hey!" he shouted again. "Stop it! Right now!"

No-Neck was cradling his hand, tiny tears starting at the corners of his eyes.

"He dented my axe!" Moone barked again, ready to lay into the kid.

Sky stared at him. It didn't seem to occur to Moone that he'd just won a fight, such as it was. Fights were probably a dime a dozen. You won them, you lost them. But messing with a guy's horn!

Sky was relieved it had ended so quickly, even if it meant the party was over and the band fired. The girl from the social committee wasn't even going to pay them, but Suze had a quiet talk with her, and then Moone threatened to sue the school for damaging his "axe." Finally, the girl just handed over the envelope filled with tens and ones. A few minutes later they were out on the street.

"Well," said Max, piling his black drum cases by the curb, "*that* was interesting."

"I can't believe you stood up to that guy," Sky said to Suze.

"You have to," she said simply, but she was smiling around the eyes. She didn't look scared, or shaken, or even angry.

"Guess they didn't go for 'Regeneration,'" said Moone.

Max gave a little laugh. "Everybody's a critic."

"I'll need fifty," Moone said suddenly.

"Wait, you agreed to forty," said Max.

"That was before some preppy asshole broke my horn."

Sky looked from one to the other. He could see Max heating up and gave him a calming nod.

"What do you mean?" said Max sharply. "He agreed to forty!"

Sky just shook his head. He wanted to be able to work with this Johnny Moone again.

"I don't know," said Max. "What do you think, Larry? It's kind of up to you and Suze."

The bass player shrugged. "Not great, but if the guy dented his axe . . ."

"Okay with me," said Suze.

In the end, Max pulled out five tens for Moone, then handed twelve dollars each to Larry, Sky, and Suze. "We'll settle the small stuff on Monday."

"Can't say it hasn't been fun," said Larry, hoisting

his bass fiddle and heading toward the subway, his Adam's apple leading the way.

"Yeah, yeah," said Max.

Seconds later a loud pop behind them made them jump, and Sky felt something sting his ankle. Shards of a bottle littered the sidewalk, and Coke was splattered everywhere. They looked up. Some guy was grinning at them from the balcony of the school's second floor.

"That sumbitch . . . ," started Moone.

Suze grabbed his arm and gave him a steady look. "He's not worth it."

Moone stared back.

"Hey, guys, help me with my gear," said Max. He glanced up nervously. "Let's get to the corner."

To the sound of jeers overhead, the kids toted their instruments the long half block to Fifth, where a Yellow cab soon pulled up. It was one of those big old taxis, with two extra fold-down seats in the back. By loading one drum case in the trunk and another up with the driver, they were able to get everything else in the backseat.

Sky said he'd walk.

"Sure? We can fit you," said Suze.

Sky noted the flash of her knees and almost changed his mind. But he just waggled his fake book at them.

"See ya around, Junior," said Moone, balancing the saxophone case on his lap; and off they went.

Sky was glad he was walking, although his cut ankle made him wince with every other step. The air was cooler than before, he noticed, the perfect time of night, when the Upper East Side gets ready to feed the cat and tuck in. Different parts of town kept such different hours. In Midtown the sidewalks would still be busy and the clubs packed, from hot spots like Sardi's and Toots Shor to dives with buzzing signs offering REAL LIVE GIRLS for twenty-five cents a dance. Down in the Village the coffeehouses and jazz dens would be loud with excitement, the narrow streets jammed with gawkers hoping to glimpse the famous beatniks they'd read about. In between lay the garment district, block after darkened block, abandoned by the day workers from Brooklyn and Queens.

It was a different darkness here on the East Side. Not abandoned, but secluded—the drawbridges drawn up, so to speak. There was something intimate about it, even about the new high-rise apartments with balconies overlooking Central Park. Sky knew a girl who lived in one of those apartments. He'd been part of a group of kids that ended up at her place after a basketball game. She had easy eyes, blue and clear. She hadn't particularly noticed him, but she was nice. She never mocked him. Which balcony was it?

Jill.

Hi up there, Jill, wherever you are.

Thinking of her made him think of Suze Matheson and of her elegant neck that he'd never seen before tonight. Why did she always dress *down?* He might want to hide sometimes, but why would Suze?

Sky hobbled to a bench and eased off his left shoe and sock. Didn't look too bad. He just hoped there wasn't any glass stuck in him. Holding the shoe in one hand, he started south along the park.

He crossed the street at Seventieth, the recently tarred macadam soft to his bare foot. The Frick Museum stood on the corner, looking both smug and lonely behind its fence of tall metal spears.

Sky limped on. *Diddle diddle dumpling,* he thought idiotically, *my son John. One shoe off and one shoe on.* Between Madison and Park were all these ritzy houses. Between Park and Lexington the houses were still pretty fancy, but you didn't have to be an actual millionaire. You could almost see the real-estate values dropping, block by block, as you walked east. Sky and his dad lived in a nice apartment on the top two floors of a four-story brownstone near Third Avenue, where the El was being torn down. The roar of the elevated trains had ceased a couple of years ago, but the structure had remained, like the skeleton of an enormous dinosaur, its spine stretching from Wall Street to the Bronx. Ugly as it was, Sky would miss it. He liked the cobblestones and Rubin's Deli and the dark little shops. Yes, and the fish market with its sawdust floor and display cases filled with ice. There was always a cool breeze, scented with fish, as you walked by.

Sky stood before his house and looked at the upper duplex, where he lived. His heart sank to see a light on in the top-floor window, his father's room.

Why couldn't he be asleep?

He sat down on the sidewalk and pulled on his sock and shoe. "Ouch!" he said aloud.

Sky slipped his key into the top and then the lower lock of the white front door. Overhead, sycamore leaves were making a soft clatter. He noticed that clouds were moving in and a breeze picking up. A leathery leaf suddenly flapped against Sky's forehead. Other leaves were scraping along the sidewalk. Rain?

The hot spell, noticeable even an hour ago, had broken like a fever. He closed his eyes and felt the cooling wind.

In a week it would be October.

A sharp pain woke him early. Sky swung his legs out of the narrow bed and looked down, frowning. The left ankle was swollen. He should have put peroxide or something on it when he got home, but he'd forgotten in the midst of dealing with his dad. Must've rained during the night, he realized, looking out at the puddles on the roof of the dry cleaner's. Above the tenements, with their crosshatched fire escapes, the sky was growing lighter. He limped to the bathroom, washed his foot gingerly with soap and warm water, then reached into the medicine cabinet. The peroxide fizzed along the dark line of the cut. He was irritated, because he couldn't disguise his limp and would have to tell his father about it. He hobbled downstairs to start the coffee.

To his surprise, he found his father already up and the kettle hissing on the stove. The old wall clock, clucking softly, pointed to 6:05.

"Hey, sport." A compact man, Quinn Schuyler had a perpetual tan reaching to the top of his round and balding head. It was an aggressive head, Sky had always thought, a head for business. The tan still surprised him, since his father didn't spend much time outdoors. A sunlamp, from a catalog, buzzed in Quinn's front room for fifteen minutes each evening. "Helps with business," Quinn had explained early on in his tanning regime. "Clients like the healthy look."

At dawn, under the fluorescent ceiling light in the narrow kitchen, Quinn didn't look healthy so much as yellow.

"What's wrong with your foot?"

"Nothing."

"You're limping. Let's see it."

Quinn poured hot water into the coffee filter while Sky reluctantly pulled off his sock. Quinn noticed the wince.

"Could be infected. We should see Stephens. How did this happen?"

There was no use trying to escape once the old bulldog got hold of a subject; but that was more talking than Sky was willing to do. He kept trying to shrug away his father's questions, but he finally had to say something about the broken bottle.

Quinn immediately wanted to know what had led up to the incident. "People don't just scale bottles at fleeing musicians."

Sky did his best to minimize the fight, but that didn't work. If his father hadn't been a manufacturer of plumbing widgets, he would have made a good prosecuting attorney. Soon he had the whole story, right down to the paltry twelve dollars Sky had hobbled home with.

Quinn turned away and poured more water into the coffee filter.

"It's nothing, Dad."

"We'll see Stephens."

"It's Saturday."

"What? Speak up."

"I said, it's Saturday."

"He owes me," Quinn replied. "I redid his sink."

Sky sighed. He did a lot of sighing around his father.

"And then we have a talk, you and me." Quinn ran a hand over his golden dome. "This isn't working out."

Oh God, thought Sky, *not another talk.*

"*Un*acceptable," Quinn continued, hanging on to the "un" for something like a whole second.

He poured two cups and set one in front of his son. Sky had been drinking coffee since he was thirteen, when his mother died. Somehow it had made him feel more solid, more *here,* at a time when the world was sliding from under his feet. Quinn didn't seem to mind or even notice that his son had taken up coffee. Probably, he didn't know about the cigarettes, which Sky never smoked around the house anyway. Quinn had left child-rearing matters up to his wife and didn't have a clue what a boy should eat. Or what he himself should eat. When you're hungry, you put food in your mouth.

Sky said something.

"What? You're going to have to speak up."

"I wasn't in the fight."

"You were there."

"I was there, yeah."

"What?"

"Nothing."

"You were where you shouldn't've been. And doing what?"

Sky didn't answer.

His father gave him a long look and slowly shook his head. "We have to talk."

Dr. Stephens saw Sky at 9:00 A.M. in his home in the East Eighties and refused to let Quinn pay for the visit. Sky was struck, as in the past, at how handsome the doctor was, in a Scandinavian way, and how resonant his voice. His neatly clipped, once-blond hair held touches, not of gray, but of white, like little patches of snow at the edge of a well-tended field. He had to be forty at least, Sky thought.

The doctor asked him, not just about his foot, but about how things were going in school and if he was a little less nervous these days.

"Sure," Sky lied. He remembered that his dad had brought him here a year ago when Sky had stopped speaking. Stephens had assumed the boy's silence was related to his mother's death. The death of a parent, he'd said, was bound to raise a lot of fears in a kid, added to the usual anxieties of adolescence. Nobody had ever said such things to Sky before. He couldn't imagine his father saying them. Life is hard, get used to it. That was Quinn's philosophy.

Looking past the doctor's shoulder, Sky noticed an archway to a dim bedroom and an unmade bed beyond. At that moment Mrs. Stephens passed by in a pale blue nightgown, brushing her hair, and it occurred to Sky suddenly that she and her husband might have been having sex when Quinn Schuyler, the round-headed widget maker, had called about his son's foot. It was a stunning thought, and he looked at the doctor with new interest. People like him, professional grown-ups with neatly vacuumed apartments, actually *did it.*

With his foot newly bandaged and a small box of pills going *chucka-chucka* in his pocket, Sky shook the doctor's hand.

"Don't hesitate to call me," said Stephens. "Anytime. You don't have to wait for your dad to drag you here." He winked at Mr. Schuyler.

"I won't," said Sky.

"Even if you just want to talk."

"I won't. I mean, I will. Thanks." He glanced briefly at the empty archway—no sign of the blue night-gown—and followed his father to the door.

"Pretty nice of him," mumbled Sky when they reached the street.

"Mn." Quinn walked east to Lex and started south. At Seventy-ninth they had to wait as a yellow bus roared by, spewing exhaust. But after it had passed, Quinn didn't cross. He just stood on the sidewalk. "Son," he said, "I want you to cut out this band thing."

Sky looked at him with alarm.

"That's right. Listen. Two things. One, it's a waste of time—"

"It is not a waste of time!"

"Funny how well I can hear you when you have something to say."

"Dad, it is not a waste of time. Jazz happens to be an art form."

"And two—"

"You can't make me."

Quinn Schuyler raised his nearly hairless eyebrows as though to see his son more clearly. "I can't make you? I can throw out the goddam piano; that'll make you."

Sky seemed to be choking. "Throw out Mom's piano?"

"Your mother is dead. She's been dead for two years. What does she care about a piano?"

Sky said nothing.

"Well, answer me!"

"You wouldn't."

"I can't hear you."

Sky forced himself to speak louder. "You wouldn't do it."

Again, Quinn raised his nonexistent brows. "You're daring me?"

Sky bit his tongue.

"I said, are you daring me?"

Sky looked down. His piano. His *one thing.* "I'll play softer," he said finally.

"What?"

"I'll play *softer.*"

"That's good, but that's not the point. The point is, you're wasting your life with that crap."

"Dad, can we cross the street?"

"No, we cannot cross the street. I'm talking to you."

People were elbowing past them, running to make the light.

"Don't do it, Dad."

Quinn looked at his son. A lady with a baby carriage pushed her way between them. "Excuse me!" she said.

"I'm asking you, Dad." Sky was chewing on his underlip.

His father seemed to be gauging his misery. "All right," he said at last.

"I can keep the piano?"

"For now. But you have to give up the band."

Sky felt stricken. He mumbled something.

"Speak up."

"I said it's not fair."

"Fair or not."

"I won't do it."

"Oh, but you will."

Sky glared but said nothing.

"*Listen* to me!" said Quinn. His voice suddenly had an edge to it. "This is no good. I know you think high school is a time to have fun; but you have to be *thinking*. You have to look *ahead*. This jazz, this is no profession. Look at you. You get your foot cut up in a fight."

"I wasn't in a—"

"I'm telling you something. Look ahead. What happens to these so-called jazz musicians you think are so hot? They turn into lowlifes. They die of booze and drugs. They play in bars."

Sky was watching the light turn from red to green.

"Your mother would say the same, if she was alive."

Still green.

"So, better to put a stop to it now, before next time they cut your throat. And don't give me that look, like I kicked your dog!"

"I don't have a dog," muttered Sky. "You kicked *me*."

His father didn't hear. He was looking around for the traffic light. "You coming or what?"

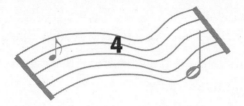

That afternoon his father gave him a crumpled twenty and sent him to get some groceries. Relieved to be on his own, Sky climbed carefully down the stairs, favoring his bandaged foot. The sun was dazzling, the breeze cool. He lifted his arm and rubbed his face against his sweatshirt, only then realizing there'd been tears in his eyes.

There was no way Sky was going to leave the band. His quitting would break the group up, which would be a major drag for Max and Larry, who needed what money they made. Not that Sky didn't.

Swinging the string-net shopping bag, he headed where he always went when he had nowhere to go: Third Avenue. There wasn't anything to see, but he liked peering in the windows of the narrow shops he already thought of as doomed. He was feeling a little doomed himself. There was the hole-in-the-wall newspaper joint that carried the comic books he used to love: *Krazy Kat, Captain Marvel, Archie & Friends.* Truth is, he still liked them; but he recently discovered the place carried other magazines as well, including a new one called *Playboy*. He'd seen a copy once at Max's house. Max had gotten it from his cousin, who was something like twenty.

Today Sky stopped in out of habit. It was part of his routine. He checked out the new issue of *Plastic Man* and bought a pack of Beech-Nut gum. His mother had liked Beech-Nut. Her purse used to smell of it.

He wandered a few doors south to the antique shop. Sky had never seen a customer in the place. Who would want brass chandeliers with dusty crystal pendants? Or sconces and brooches—all that junk? Still, it was calming to squint through the reflections of traffic into the gloom and see, in the back, the bare bulb over the desk and Mr. Wood himself, dry as a stick, going over his invoices. The old guy looked up and gave a little wave.

Sky headed to Winter's Market on Seventy-first. He'd gone there often with his mother and watched her pick the best stew meat and the freshest greens. Nell Schuyler had been quite a particular woman, in her soft-spoken way. Now it was up to him to do the shopping. What did his weirdly tanned, bullheaded father know about romaine? If it were up to him, he'd order in Chinese every night. Sky wasn't a whiz at cooking, but he'd begun to learn, out of self-defense.

From there, he went down a few stores to Rubin's Deli. The stone steps up to the jingling door had been climbed so often for so many years that they had little bowl-shaped hollows in them. *That's a lot of shoe leather,* he thought, fitting his sneakers into the depressions.

Dave Rubin was one of the few tradesmen who actually talked to him. Sky answered, too, though not always audibly. Dave and his brother, Irv, had been fond of Sky's mother and often mentioned her.

"How's the piano, kid?" said Rubin, glancing at the scale suspended before him. He was weighing liverwurst for a frizzy-haired woman.

Sky compressed his lips into a smile. "Good," he said.

"You play any Bach? I like Bach. Soothes the noives."

"Brubeck."

"Don't know the gentleman."

"His name is Dave too. Dave Brubeck." Sky liked this Dave Rubin, old and sallow-skinned though he was, with age blotches above his cheekbones.

"Ya know," said Rubin, wrapping the wurst in waxed paper, "I used to be an artist." He pronounced the word "awtist." Pulling the stub of a pencil from behind his ear, he scribbled a price.

"Really?"

Rubin handed the wurst to the lady, who paid Rubin's wife.

"This was years ago. I decided I would make my

matzoh balls with raisins in them. Interesting idea, don't you think?"

Sky nodded cautiously.

"Sheila thought so too." He leaned confidentially over the counter. "They didn't sell." He shook his head, his cheeks wobbling. "So much for awt."

Sky snickered.

"He laughs. You should laugh the next time you have six dozen raisin matzoh balls that nobody wants."

"You sound like my father."

"What?"

"I said, you sound like my father."

"Sounds like a smawt man."

"Uh-huh."

Rubin looked at him. "I guess I said the wrong thing. That's all right, I'm always saying the wrong thing. Ask Sheila." He wiped his hands on his white apron, which was not white. "Here," he said, "have a dill."

Rubin drew a large pickle from a jar, cradled it in waxed paper, and handed it to him. He did this every time Sky came in.

"Thanks, Mr. Rubin."

Sky bought some kaiser rolls, sliced Swiss, and a quarter pound of bologna. His father's favorite lunch. Somehow things seemed a little better after seeing

Dave Rubin. Sky bit into the pickle as he cut a diagonal under the shadow of the El and headed home.

The phone jangled. *Who would be calling at nine o'clock at night?*

"If it's for me, I'm dead," Quinn called down the stairs, then disappeared into his room. Sky picked up in the living room.

"Hey." It was Max's voice.

"Hey."

"Guess who's at Birdland."

Sky was silent.

"Basie," Max supplied. "He's got that new kid, Sonny Payne, on drums."

This was big. Payne was the fastest thing on two sticks. It was also irrelevant. "Last time I checked," Sky mumbled, "we were fifteen."

"We can try."

That was Max. Sky had to admit his "Hi-there-beautiful" approach had gotten him through many doors in the past. So far no nightclubs.

"Also, I'm in trouble," said Sky, remembering.

"Whatcha do? Play a tune loud enough for him to actually hear it?"

"Long story."

"Can't you get out tonight?"

Sky shook his head, then realized he was on the

phone. "Don't see how," he said. His father would never let him go prowling around the city, not by himself and certainly not with Max the Bad Influence.

Max was silent.

Sky was silent.

Then Max was silent some more. This was really putting on the pressure, because Max was never silent.

"Wish I could," murmured Sky.

Max started reciting in a singsongy voice: "Sky climbed down from his bare tree this year . . ."

Sky chuckled.

". . . and ran away . . ."

"Okay."

". . . to where there were no Quinn Schuyler Christmas trees . . ."

"I get it."

Max was silent again.

Sky let out a sigh. "How about eleven fifteen, at the corner?"

"You're shittin' me."

"If I'm not there by twenty after, I couldn't make it." He hung up and immediately felt dizzy, a sensation he recognized as fear. He knew his dad always headed to his room at precisely 10:45 to read and do paperwork before lights-out. Not to mention his fifteen minutes under the sunlamp. But the stairs between the fourth and third floors were prone to creaks, and the door to their apartment made a huge *ka-chunk!* when you pulled it closed, no matter how careful you were.

Not to mention the fact that they'd never get in to Birdland.

Sky hurried to his room to check the money jar in the top drawer of his bureau. Several rolled-up fives, a lot of change, and—lucky day—the twelve dollars from the dance at Keller.

He checked his watch. Too early to change. It would look suspicious to be seen kicking around the apartment at 9:00 P.M. in a fresh pair of khakis and a button-down shirt. Sky took his good stuff down to the third floor and stashed it in the hall closet, near the door.

Two hours to kill. He went to the living room and opened the record cabinet. Besides the classics his mother had loved, there was an impressive number of jazz LPs—Sky's own collection—piano jazz, mostly, ranging from the stride piano of Earl Hines to the latest releases of Bill Evans and Thelonious Monk. He had all five of Art Olmedo's obtainable records. He pulled out the latest and lowered it gently onto the turntable, making sure the volume was turned well down. His dad's bedroom was directly overhead.

Olmedo's playing filled the room with abrupt angles and primary colors. Sky had never come across such a combination of confidence and recklessness in a jazz player. And yet the guy was blind, lost his sight at age three or something. How could he play that way and not see what he's doing?

That's what I want, Sky thought. *I want some of that.*

"Alec! Don't you have any homework to do this weekend?" Quinn Schuyler was leaning over the banister.

Sky, who hated his first name, went out in the hall so he could talk to his dad in a normal voice. "Some."

"Maybe you should be doing it."

"Is the music too loud?"

"What?"

"Too loud?"

"It's always too loud, especially when your homework isn't done. You know the rules."

Sky knew the rules. Work first, play later. There was no use arguing that playing music made the work go faster, especially this weekend, when he was supposed to study for next week's world geography midterm. He turned down the hi-fi till it was barely audible, then sat at the blond upright piano and shadow-played— ran his fingers over the keyboard without pressing down hard enough to make the notes sound. He was trying to keep up with Olmedo, but half the time he couldn't even tell what key the guy was in, he switched around so often. It helped, at such moments, to glance up at the oil painting over the piano—a favorite of his mom's. It wasn't a masterpiece or anything, but Sky liked it. It showed a woodcutter trudging up a snowy hill with a load of firewood strapped to his back. That's the way it felt sometimes, practicing, only Sky was carrying a piano. It didn't seem he'd *ever* get up that hill.

After awhile he went to the kitchen for a snack. The clock had hardly moved since the last time he'd checked. He opened his scuffed leather briefcase and pulled out a fat notebook and a fatter textbook. A half hour later he still didn't know Quemoy from Matsu, although, since he was sitting at the kitchen table, he managed to consume half a package of Oreos.

"Alec?"

Sky went out to the hall and looked up. His father's head peered down at him like a harvest moon. "Whatcha doing, sport?"

"Geography."

"That's good. I want to talk to you, if you got a minute."

"What is it?"

"Well, come up here. Don't make me yell."

You'll end up yelling anyway, Sky thought, starting up the stairs.

His father preceded him into the bedroom and sat down in the antique rocker, one of the few furnishings left over from the time when this had been his mother's room. The Persian rug was another reminder, although Sky had the feeling his dad would have preferred a bare floor. He went for the minimal look and had cleared away the family pictures and the sentimental print of a girl and her dog that had hung for years over the bed. After Nell's death Quinn had painted the blue walls white, turning the bedroom into something resembling an office.

"Sit," he said. "I wanted to follow up."

Sky dawdled beside the rolling desk chair, but didn't sit down.

"I might have been a little rough this afternoon."

Sky looked at his father. An apology?

"There's some stuff you don't know," Quinn went on. "Sit."

Sky circled the chair and finally lowered himself into it. He rolled a few inches back and forth while his father tilted in the rocker.

"First off," said Quinn, "I'm fine. Great shape. Except I got high blood pressure."

Sky had heard about high blood pressure. "Is it serious?"

"Serious, no. It means my blood's in too much of a hurry to get around my body, that's all."

"Oh."

"But."

Sky could have done without the dramatic pauses.

He watched the gleam of the desk lamp on his father's head.

"I gotta be careful. Remember when I was in Milwaukee for a few days last month? I wasn't in Milwaukee, I was in Lenox Hill."

"What!"

"It's nothing. I didn't want to worry you."

"You were in the *hospital*?"

"It's all right. They gave me medicine."

"For your blood pressure."

"Yeah, and, you know, for my heart."

Oh my God, thought Sky.

"I'm all right, but you need to know where I keep this medicine, so in case there's some emergency, which there *won't* be . . ."

Oh my God.

"Don't look at me like that!"

"Dad . . ."

"I knew I shouldn't have told you."

"No, no."

"Anyway, I keep it in the top drawer of that chest by the door. Take a look, so you know."

Sky went to the chest. There was a little white container with a pharmacy number.

"See it there? So you can get it if you have to."

Sky nodded.

"Maybe that's why I got less patience these days."

Less?

"I got all this stuff on my mind. And trying to get you raised. It's a serious world out there, and you're going to have to learn how to live in it. Right now, I'm sorry to say, you wouldn't have a chance in hell. You don't even *talk* to people like a normal person."

What was his father saying? That he was going to die?

"I want you to get your feet on the ground. I want you to get a start in the right direction. I want you," said Quinn, pitching forward in the rocking chair, "to quit wasting your damn time!"

"I'm not—" Sky stopped himself. That line of argument didn't work.

"So." Quinn clapped his hands on his knees. "No more of this foolishness with the band. I'm not saying you have to go into *my* business—although, God knows, it's a good business. Think about it, Alec. People will always need toilets."

Sky said something.

"What? You gotta speak up."

"People will always need music."

Quinn shook his head. "Go," he said, "get out of here. What are you going to do? Work on geography?"

"I thought I'd do some laundry."

"You sure you want to go down in the basement? It's after eleven."

"I'll bring a book."

Quinn let out a sigh. "Suit yourself. I'm turning in. Think about what I said."

"I will."

"Do that." He reached over and gave his son a playful cuff on the cheek.

Sky stood in the third-floor hallway. 11:38. No sound from upstairs. Now or never. Probably, Max had already stopped waiting for him.

He let himself out of the apartment and started down to the front hall. Halfway down he stopped to change into his good clothes, suddenly fearful that someone would come out of the lower apartment and find him with his pants down. He zipped the khakis and slipped his arms into his blue shirt. The cleaner sure liked the starch. The shirt was so stiff he could hardly button the thing. He shrugged into his blue blazer, then balled up his old clothes and stuffed them into a shopping bag, stowing the bag under the stairwell by the cellar door. He paused to check himself in the big mirror over the mail table. The blazer looked smart enough, but he still looked like a teenager. He had yet to put a razor to his cheek. Max had. He could even claim that he *needed* to shave. He was as early in this puberty business as Sky was late. A clothes tree stood by the table, with several hats perched on it, all belonging to the guy who lived in the downstairs apartment. Sky picked a brown fedora. At least it threw his face into shadow.

Stepping outside, he immediately lost control of the hat. He ran and grabbed it before the wind blew it into the street.

Heading toward Third Avenue, he glanced back, his stomach sinking to see an unnatural blue light in the top window. The sunlamp. Suddenly, Sky felt inexpressibly sad. His dad was getting his fifteen minutes of imitation sunlight so he would look healthy for his clients. Did he think that would help him sell more drain stoppers?

And Sky had just lied to him.

He should go back. They could have a conversation, play a game of gin rummy, maybe. They used to do that, when Sky's mom was alive. And Chinese checkers. They'd had good times. Or was he just remembering what he wanted to? The truth was, Quinn could never sit still, and his restlessness grew worse as the business expanded. He saw life as a series of irritations, and Sky was the most irritating grain of sand in the whole oyster. If his dad ever found out about tonight . . .

Sky reached the corner, holding the brim of his hat to keep it from flying off. It was eerie out here under the half-dismantled Elevated tracks. Most of the upper deck was gone, and the massive posts cast Stonehenge-like shadows under the streetlamps. From behind one of them appeared a pinpoint of orange light. Then a muffled figure stepped out, the collar of his raincoat turned up to deflect the wind.

Max tossed his cigarette into the shadows. "I almost gave up on you."

"Sorry."

"Trouble getting out?"

Sky waggled his hand.

The friends were silent as they walked to the Sixty-eighth Street subway and waited for the IRT. The train took its time arriving, as always this late at night.

"Dad wants me to quit the band."

Max stared. *"Why?"*

"Thinks musicians are lowlifes."

It was unusual to find Max at a loss for words. He stared at the tracks. A brown rat ducked under the third rail. "What are you going to do?"

"Don't know."

"Sky, jazz is your *life.* Doesn't he understand that?"

Actually, Sky didn't understand it himself. Was it true? He knew he loved jazz. He thought about it all the time, except, of course, whenever a girl happened to cross his line of vision. He practiced hours a day, often soundlessly, after his dad was asleep. He wrote out chord changes from records that he listened to over and over, until they were too scratched to play. He'd even brought his little composition book with him tonight, just in case.

Did that mean jazz was his life?

A distant shower of sparks announced the train's approach. It groaned to a stop, swallowed them up, shook them around for five minutes, and then dumped them out at Fifty-first Street. They headed west on foot.

The club was near the corner of Fifty-second Street and Seventh Avenue. It would have been easy to miss the place. A modest awning sported the word BIRDLAND and the slogan JAZZ CORNER OF THE WORLD, but there were no bright lights or marquee. Sky gazed warily at the doorman—or was he a bouncer?—standing beside a placard that announced simply, BASIE'S BACK.

Max glanced at Sky, then paused to pull the fedora farther down over his friend's face. "Let me do the talking," he said.

They passed the first hurdle without talking at all. Collars up, they sauntered past the doorman, who obligingly held the door. A drumroll and the wail of a saxophone echoed weirdly up the staircase as Sky and Max descended to the basement club. Muffled trumpets led to a crash of cymbals and smattered applause.

An admission booth barred their way at the foot of the stairs. Sky's heart was going pretty good as Max pulled out his wallet and smiled nonchalantly at the large black woman behind the window.

"Hello, beautiful," he said. "Two, please."

The woman just stared at him.

Max cleared his throat and extracted several wrinkled five-dollar bills. "How much?"

The woman might have been a statue of the Buddha.

Max cleared his throat again. He had to speak loudly because the band had just swung into a new number. "Two admissions? How much?"

The woman turned and called out to someone, "Clayton, you want to see this!"

Sky started backing away, ready to scramble up the stairs.

"What seems to be the matter, miss?" Max's casual air would have been more convincing if his voice hadn't cracked just then. The band suddenly went soft as the piano took a solo.

That's Basie playing, Sky realized.

"Clayton!"

Max was shifting from one foot to the other. This Clayton character might be a bruiser who'd roust them out the door or deliver them to the police. Instead, a high-pitched voice called out, *"Hole own, womma!"* And then the smallest, roundest, darkest person Sky had ever seen—man or woman, he couldn't tell—parted the curtains to the club proper and rolled up to the booth.

The big woman jerked her head toward Max and Sky. "These boys are tryin' to get inta Birdlan'. Whaddya think?"

Clayton squinted at them, then shook his (her?) head and chuckled. "Seemsa me, they took a wrong toin. Soda shop's two blocks *that* way!"

The voice, Sky decided, was falsetto, not soprano. Clayton was a man.

"Actually," said Max, improvising a new approach, "we're students. We have a band of our own. That's the truth."

"And you're, what, fourteen years old?" said the woman in the booth.

Max looked insulted. He drew himself up to his full height. "We're seventeen."

"Uh-huh." She winked at Clayton. "But the sign say you gotta be eighteen."

A man grabbed the curtain aside. "Peewee," he said to Clayton. "You're on."

"Ole right." Clayton looked at the boys. He noticed the music composition book in Sky's hand. "An' you wan' hear Bill Basie, I s'pose."

"And Sonny Payne," said Max. "I'm the drummer."

"Hey, Peewee!"

"Comin'!" The little round man tugged on the collar of his tuxedo shirt. "Ole right," he said to the woman. "They can sit inna back. They can drink Cokes, but that's it." He disappeared through the curtain.

The ticket lady shook her head. "You heard 'im. You try to order anything else, you'll find yo sad selves right back on the street."

Sky couldn't believe it. *We're in!* he thought with a giggle as a young black man led them down a short hallway into a low-ceilinged room filled with the joyful braying of trumpets and the swerving of saxophones, all carried along by the drummer's mighty commotion. The sound was crisp, brazen, and unbelievably loud. If Sky ever played music even half this loud at home, the windows would rattle out of their frames! That old sunlamp would explode!

The stage was bright, with light bouncing off the upraised horns and gleaming drums, even the starched white cuffs of Count Basie, the Man Himself, sitting at the piano and grinning, hitting an occasional *plink, plink, plink* up near the top of the keyboard.

The rest of the club was so dark, Sky and Max couldn't see where they were stumbling. They were shown to an imitation-leather bench at the back of the hall, and a little table was set before them, lit vaguely by an orange ceiling light.

"I hear you gentlemen would like to sample our selection of Coca-Colas," said the waiter, deadpan.

"That's right," said Max, his spirits high. "Bring us your best." The man slipped off into the darkness. "Spare no expense!" He punched Sky on the arm. "We made it, buddy!"

"Yeah."

"Hey!"

"Yeah."

The waiter didn't return for half an hour, but that was fine with Sky. With his composition book held up to the dim light, he scribbled frantically to catch the chord changes.

Max didn't try to write, but he was listening hard, especially during Sonny Payne's one-hundred-mile-an-hour drum solo. Sometimes Max would rap his fingers on the tabletop, but then he'd just smile and shake his head.

The band finally took a break, and the lights came up a bit, enough for Sky to see that the notes he'd scribbled were illegible. That didn't bother him so much. It was the electric, firsthand connection that mattered.

Before long Sky looked up to see a small round figure in a dazzling white shirt step out on the left side of the bandstand. It was Peewee, or Clayton, or whatever he called himself.

"Ladies and gennelmen!" the little man called out, his sharp falsetto cutting through the smoke, "Birdland takes a great deal of pride in presenting to you at this time . . . Joe Williams!"

The hoots and applause were drowned out by the Basie rhythm section setting up a swinging beat for a tall black man in a camel-colored tux who stepped to center stage, took firm hold of the mike, and let loose a rich, throaty baritone.

"Well, *all right!*" the man shouted. "*Okay!* You *win!* I'm in love with *you!*"

The saxes joined the rolling background while trumpets punched out the offbeats. Several of the sidemen began shouting encouragement, as if the band or Williams needed it. Sky was swept away.

Something was beginning to bother him, though. Maybe it was the blue fluorescent light indicating the exit sign, but Sky suddenly remembered the glow of his father's sunlamp, in the top window of the house.

"What time is it?"

"Huh?" Max was in a jazz dreamworld.

Sky tapped his wrist.

"One fifteen."

"My God. I better get home."

"There's one more set."

But Sky's stomach was already doing unpleasant things. He touched Max's shoulder. "Need to go now."

Max nodded.

They split the tab and climbed the steep stairs to the street. The breeze was colder, and a hint of rain dampened the air.

"Let's find a cab," Sky said. "We'll get there faster."

Max looked at him curiously. "Okay, boss."

With no traffic to slow them, the taxi soared up Central Park West to Sixty-fifth and cut through the park. Three minutes later they were rolling east along Seventieth.

"First stop on the left," Sky called out. The cab pulled over.

"Was that a gas?" Max said, shaking his head.

"It was great. Really great." Sky peered out at the house. The top window was dark. *Thank God,* he thought. *He's been asleep after all.*

"See you Monday," Max said, giving Sky's shoulder a light punch.

The taxi pulled away, and Sky slid his key into the lock.

It was dark in the vestibule. Tossing the fedora on the hat stand, Sky headed behind the stairwell where he'd stashed his clothes.

Wait. Where were they? He clicked on the hall light. He distinctly remembered leaving the shopping bag beside the cellar door.

Nothing!

Sky tried to think, but panic was making his mind skip like a nicked record. *All right,* he thought. *All right, here's what it is: The downstairs tenant took it in. Or took it down to the washing machine. Or thought it was trash and tossed it.*

Sky hustled down the wooden stairs into the low basement. No sign of his clothes anywhere. Now his heart was pumping hard. Racing back from the cellar, he rounded the turn of the stairs and headed up toward his apartment, taking the steps two at a time.

"Looking for something?"

Sky's knees buckled.

Vague light revealed half of a man's face looking down at him from the landing.

There sat Quinn Schuyler in his yellow pajamas, a shopping bag between his knees. As Sky watched, appalled, Quinn extracted a pair of dungarees and then a sweatshirt. He kept staring at Sky, his eyes small and hard, as he let the clothes drop on the floor. Then he balled up the bag and let that drop too. It rolled partway down the stairs.

Without a word, he stood and went into the apartment.

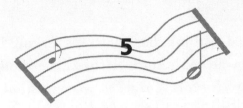

5

Tuesday afternoon two large men, one in a greasy conductor's cap, stumped up the stairs carrying ropes and padding.

"In here, gentlemen." Quinn Schuyler tilted his head toward the living room.

Traitor, thought Sky.

Five minutes later the little piano was upended, swathed in blankets, lashed with rope, and wheeled into the hallway. Soon you could hear the wheels of the dolly bumping downstairs, the sound growing fainter. Sky looked out the front window. A truck with the sign MOISHE'S MOVERS emblazoned on the side stood double-parked. Finally, the men appeared on the sidewalk. Quinn was down there with them, gesturing, signing the papers, handing out tips. He was joking with them! Sky couldn't believe it. He stared at his father's round body foreshortened by distance and thought of a big bug. He turned away in disgust.

Across the room the oil painting hung over the strangely empty place where the piano had stood. Sharp dents pocked the rug, and tiny thunderheads of dust lay along the wall. There was his pen! He also found a dime and a penny. In a daze he rubbed the coins between his fingers as if they held a secret meaning. An idea was taking form in his mind. It was more emotion than idea, and it came into focus as a single explosive word: *No!*

He heard footsteps on the stairs. Sky hated the sound. He hated the heavy brown shoes making that sound. He hated the feet in those shoes.

"So!" said Quinn, bursting in. He was breathing hard, his face red with exertion.

Sky would not look at him.

"Now you know I mean what I say." Quinn held the back of a chair to steady himself while he got his breath back. "The people who work for me know this. Now my son knows it. You don't lie to me and think that nothing is going to happen."

Sky slid onto the sofa and started toying with a round coaster on the side table. *I have nothing to say to this man,* he thought.

"Did you think I wouldn't find out?"

Sky turned the coaster on its edge and twirled it slowly.

"Speak to me!"

I have nothing to say to this man.

"Put that thing down!"

Sky let the coaster circle noisily to a stop.

Quinn was breathing hard again, as if he'd climbed an extra flight of stairs. "That's it!" he barked, in a voice probably louder than he intended. "Your band is finished. Your piano is finished. And now you get to do nothing for the next week except come home and do your homework. You got that?"

Sky looked up.

"That's right. You are grounded, mister."

Sky nodded, his face expressionless.

His father's face, however, was a contortion. "You have nothing to say?"

Sky picked up the coaster again and began twirling it.

Abruptly, Quinn strode from the room, climbed the stairs to his room, and slammed the door.

Do I have anything to say?

As a matter of fact, I do. I have one word: No.

No, I will not stop playing. No, I will not break up the band. Do what you want, I don't care.

He flung the coaster across the room. It hit the painting and bounced away, leaving a two-inch gash in the canvas.

Oh no! The painting had been his mother's favorite and, lately, his own as well. Tears sprouted in his eyes. Grabbing his keys, he barged down the stairs, yanked open the front door, and raced into the blinding street.

♪

Next day in study hall Suze came over and slid into the chair two desks away. Students were spaced at every other desk to discourage whispering, but expert whisperers like Suze could get around that. She'd gotten the piano story from Max, but even without it she knew something was different. Sky was always quiet, but now he was silent, even with friends.

"Hey," she whispered.

He looked up, startled to see her practically right next to him.

"I need some help," she said. "I'm looking for a friend of mine. Maybe you've seen him? His name's Sky."

He gave a half smile in spite of himself.

"Could we have a little quiet in the back?" called the birdlike Miss DeGraw from her desk at the front.

Suze ducked her head slightly and gave Sky one of her secret smiles.

"He's not much fun these days," Sky murmured.

"Oh, sure he is," she whispered. "Do you think I could get to see him later? I need to talk to him."

He knew she was trying to cheer him up. He had nothing against that. Who wouldn't give a girl like Suze the chance to cheer him up?

"Let's do our own work back there," cawed Miss DeGraw; but Sky knew that if she were really hot under her doily-like collar, her voice would have turned thin and gone up half an octave. It was still within human range, which meant she recognized one of the whisperers as the well-brought-up, absolutely straight-A, and perfectly beautiful Susan Matheson.

Suze bent her head to scribble in her notebook. Her long hair slid down, covering half her face, and Sky caught the faint scent of shampoo. She watched for her chance and then pushed the page in front of him: "Sixth-period break?"

He puffed out his breath in a sigh.

"Come on," she whispered.

He wrote back, "Okay."

When sixth period arrived the doors blasted open and the hordes raced into the courtyard, determined to make the most of their fifteen minutes of freedom. Girls made high-speed fashion observations, full of Oh Gods, while boys shoved one another and shouted to friends. Sky and Suze kept to the edge, circling past the fire escape to the white fence separating the Upper School from the Lower. Sky leaned on his elbows, staring over the fence, his back to her.

"Missed you at lunch," she said.

He nodded.

"Where'd you go?"

"Around the neighborhood."

She gave him a surprised look. Kids weren't supposed to stroll out of school when they felt like it and
take walks around the neighborhood. Especially this
neighborhood.

"So you didn't get any lunch?"

He didn't answer.

"I heard about the piano," she said.

He slowly turned around. He said something.

"Sorry, it's loud out here," she said.

"I said, I'm not giving up the band."

"Of course you're not. You're way too good."

He shook his head. "Not yet."

"No, I thought you were great last Friday. Really
good."

He had to smile. "Not everybody thought so."

"They were jerks."

"Speaking of which," he murmured, suddenly aware
of a tall, sandy-haired kid coming up fast.

"Hey, Suze! Got a minute?"

It was Steve Glass, looking sporty in his tan chinos
and bicep-gripping short-sleeved sport shirt.

"Well! Steve!"

He cocked his head to the side and grinned. "I
wanted to catch you before the bell." He took no notice
of Sky's presence. "You know the Winter Dance in
December? What do you say?"

She smiled sunnily. "What do I say to what?"

"Going with me!"

"Ah, yes," she said slowly, "I'd love to, Steve, but Sky has already asked me."

He and Glass looked equally astonished.

"Who? Jabbers?" Glass gave a short laugh. "I didn't know he could talk."

"Oh," said Suze, "he can be eloquent."

Glass gaped. Maybe "eloquent" was too hard a word. "Really!" he said.

"But thank you for asking."

"Uh, yeah." He began to back up. "Sure." He threw Sky a puzzled frown, then headed back into the crowd. As he approached a group of girls his walk turned jaunty.

"He's not used to being turned down," Sky said.

"You don't mind, do you?" she said quickly. "He caught me by surprise."

"Mind?"

"Really, you don't have to take me."

He laughed. He didn't *have* to take Susan Matheson to the Winter Dance!

"What?" she said. Her eyes were uncertain. "I'm not sure I like it when you laugh."

"I was going to say, you don't have to go with *me*."

"I want to. Why wouldn't I?"

He didn't try to answer that.

"Deal?" She smiled like a conspirator.

"And what is so funny?" It was Max, bustling toward them.

"You are!" Suze gave him a shove.

He looked from one to the other. "Look," said Max, "this guy needs somewhere to practice."

"He does," she agreed.

"Well, for now he's got my place."

"Hey, thanks." Sky thought of the little, out-of-tune spinet piano at the Rosens' house, with its four and a half octaves. It was an impossible instrument, but better than pretend-playing on the kitchen table, which is what he did last night for half an hour.

"I have my drum set. We can practice. My mom doesn't mind."

Then Sky remembered. "You know I'm grounded this week."

"I thought of that. That's why I volunteered us to put on a music assembly."

"What!"

"It's a school function, and you'll have to practice for it." Max winked. "A *lot*!"

The word "chutzpah" crossed Sky's mind again. "You volunteered us to put on an assembly?"

"The fix is in."

"When?"

"We left that indefinite."

"And you think my dad will fall for it?"

"Old Crowder fell for it. Why shouldn't your father?"

"You don't know him. I take that back. You do know him."

"That's why I didn't make a definite date. We need to think beyond this week. You might have to practice after school for *months.*"

"Dad's smarter than that."

Suze was looking back and forth between them. There was happiness in her eyes. Max had gotten Sky talking again!

Just then the bell rang, a raucous clang that would put any fire station on alert. Groans could be heard as the kids began heading inside for the last two periods of the day.

"I'm still working on it," said Max as they started in. "Meanwhile, I got Miss Dowell to give your dad a call."

"What!"

"To get his permission."

"What did you tell her?"

"The truth, mostly. Your father doesn't want you taking time from your studies to play the piano."

"My God!"

"It's better than a note. You can forge a note. But a call from the school's *secretary*, that's a whole 'nother thing."

They were in the hallway now, about to split up for different classes. Suze went up and gave Max a hug—and she was not a hugger. "*You're* a whole 'nother thing."

Max looked from one to the other. "This is true," he said. He gave a little wave and headed to French.

Sky watched him go, then watched Suze heading up the stairs to the home ec classroom, her ankles flashing. He smiled. Friends.

December arrived in a cold rain, slow and steady. Above the dry cleaner's the skeleton of the half-demolished El gleamed wetly. Not a night to go out. Not a night to disobey his father again.

But there it was in the *Village Voice:* Art Olmedo himself. Rare appearance. The Red Turnip, that little club on West Fourth. This was his last night. You had to be a jazz nut to have even heard of the guy, but if you knew about him, you realized what a thing this was. "The master," as some people were calling him, had basically stopped playing in public three years ago. An article last year in *Down Beat* called him a recluse.

It would be hopeless for Sky to ask permission to go. It was hopeless in any case. They'd never let him in the club, with or without Max, and he wasn't inviting Max. Why get them both in trouble?

It had been two months since Quinn had squelched the idea of the music assembly, but Sky was still upset to think about it. He and his father had been arguing during dinner about a grade in geometry; so when

Miss Dowell called with news about the school's music assembly, Quinn was already in a mood. She had a carrying voice that Sky could've heard across the room, even if his father hadn't been holding the receiver away from his ear. He watched his dad's face redden as Dowell went on about "those talented boys" and her hopes—shared by Principal Crowder—that Alec would be allowed to practice for the event.

Quinn was not impolite. He wasn't polite, either, just brief. He said he'd get back to her with his decision the next day. It wasn't that he needed time to think about it; he just wanted to know what nonsense his son had been up to.

"Nothing, Dad. They just asked us."

"Out of the blue."

"Everybody knows we have a band."

"*Had* a band."

Sky was silent.

"*Had* a band," his father repeated. "I thought we'd gotten that straight."

"It would just be this one time."

"Not that you have a piano to practice on anyway."

"Max has one. A little one."

"Oh?"

Sky immediately realized he shouldn't have spoken.

"And how often have you been going over there to practice on this little piano of his?" Quinn ran his hand over his gleaming head. Sky had learned to fear that gesture. It meant he was figuring.

"Once or twice."

"Since I will be calling his parents, you might as well tell me."

"There's only his mother."

"What?"

"Not parents. Parent."

"I asked how often you've gone over there."

"A few times, since . . ."

"Yes. Since." He let that sit for a while. "And do you know why we got rid of our piano?"

"You don't want me to play?"

"I don't want you to *lie.*" He let that sit awhile too. "You were being punished for lying."

Suddenly, Sky really didn't understand. "Dad," he said, "you could have taken away my allowance. You could have done a lot of things. Parents tell their kids they're grounded. No movies for a week. They don't take away the *one thing*—"

"I wanted to make an impression."

Sky stared at his half-eaten dinner.

"But what's the point," Quinn continued, "if you're going to sneak off and play somebody else's piano?"

Sky looked up in alarm.

"I'm sorry, son. I will call up your friend's mother and tell her I do not want you playing that piano."

"But I need to. For the *assembly*."

"What assembly? There is no assembly."

No assembly. Unbelievable. Sky got up and left the kitchen without a word.

Now Sky stood in the dark hallway listening outside his father's door. A vague diffusion of gray filtered through the skylight over the stairs. The only sound, apart from the moan of a cab, was heavy breathing, half snore, half sigh.

He started down to the living room. By leaning most of his weight on the banister, he was able to minimize the creaking stairs. At the bottom he paused. Through the window, a streetlight flung the wild shadows of a wind-tossed sycamore. It was just an optical effect, he knew, that made the rain seem to encircle the street-lamp like a glistening spiderweb. Bony branches gleamed and swayed. The black street shone.

Glancing around the room, he suddenly gasped as a dim figure appeared before him, staring into his eyes. Then he sighed, recognizing his own image. He shouldn't be doing this. It was a form of lying to sneak out, and he didn't think of himself as a liar. Even the face in the mirror disapproved. He glanced at the ceiling. His father was upstairs asleep, trusting that his son was home, maybe taking a glass of milk from the fridge and a coconut cookie from the canister before heading to bed.

Sky slipped on his windbreaker and long red-and-black scarf, then went to the door. With the care of a safecracker, he turned the handle and pulled it toward him, holding his breath until he had stepped out onto the landing. Now came the tricky part, because the safety lock had a way of snapping closed with a sound like a double gunshot. He slipped the cardboard cover of his composition book between the lock and doorjamb. Gently, he pulled the door closed, flinching as the bolt thudded against the cardboard. Someone who was awake would have heard it; but it would not waken a distant sleeper. Sky withdrew the cover, and the door clicked.

Free! He hurried down the stairs, his scarf flying, and grabbed a fedora from the hat stand. In another moment he was outside in the rain. By the time he reached the subway, he was pretty wet. He stood a long time on the empty platform breathing the peculiar smell of damp clothes. Then the train came, and all the way downtown he avoided the eyes of the only other passenger, a filthy, wild-haired man sorting through a plastic bag. He was kind of a young guy, Sky realized. It was spooky the way he kept looking over as if he expected Sky to recognize him.

Sorry, I don't think you're one of my classmates.

Out at Waverly Place, Sky headed west and south, cutting diagonally across Washington Square. The rain was light but had an edge to it. He ducked down MacDougal Street, catching a whiff of espresso from a coffeehouse near the corner. Then there it was: the Red Turnip.

Sky pulled up his collar and gave a tug to his hat, but couldn't bring himself to reach for the door handle. He stood listening to muffled piano chords, rain ticking against the sign, and the groan of a bus over on Sixth Avenue. Then a car flew past, its tires sizzling on the wet pavement.

Sky pulled the hat brim lower for luck and opened the door. Warm air engulfed him, filled with cigarette smoke and the suddenly louder sounds of a piano trio playing a tune Sky recognized, full of Olmedo's dented chords. There was the master himself, or at least his back, curving over the keyboard.

"What is it, kid?" A large white person stood by the cash drawer. He did not have a friendly look. Even the shape of his head, thought Sky, wide in the cheeks, narrowing as it reached the stubbly crew cut, was not what you'd call sympathetic.

"I—I'd like one admission." Sky was looking down, to keep his face as much as possible in shadow.

"Can't hear you."

"One admission."

"What?"

Sky held out a ten-dollar bill. The man looked at it

as if he'd never seen anything like it. "Come back in a few years." His bony head jerked toward the door.

"No, really. I'm a student."

"What? Speak up."

"Music student! I need to listen to this and take notes." He held up his composition book as if it were a passport.

The man gave a grunt of a laugh. "That's a new one." He motioned again with his head. "Out!"

"I'd sit in the back. I wouldn't drink anything. I'd just—"

The man took a step toward him, and Sky backed up. A moment later he was in the rain.

"Okay," he said to the closed door, "that was interesting." He stood shivering until he remembered the coffeehouse around the corner and made his way to it.

The espresso shop was a different world. A bearded guy with a harmonica rigged up next to his mouth was strumming a twelve-string guitar and singing "The Water Is Wide," interrupted now and then by the roar of the coffee grinder and the whine of steam in a pitcher of milk.

Sky ordered an espresso, something he'd had a couple of times before with Max during their tramps around the Village. When it arrived, he held the little cup with both hands, to warm himself. The place was not crowded, just a few couples more interested in themselves than the music. Sky opened his comp book. At the top of a blank page he wrote, *Circle of Rain.* He wasn't sure what he was doing, but began jotting musical notes, a downward-spiraling circle of fifths. *Repeat X 6*, he wrote next to it. No bass line at all yet. He was thinking of the streetlight outside his living room, the way the rain seemed to encircle it, holding the pattern and yet moving constantly. There was music in that.

He spent twenty minutes scribbling, beginning to fit a low melody line beneath the repeated pattern in the right hand. Finally, he looked over what he'd done and shook his head. He could use help. Max was fine to bounce ideas off of, but he needed . . . He sighed. He needed Art Olmedo, is who he needed. Someone who *knew.*

Sky paid the cashier and shrugged on his jacket, now partly dry. Outside the rain had dwindled to mist. Sky turned the corner. A couple was just leaving the Turnip, the man opening an umbrella over his date, a young woman with a dancing laugh. Sky's envy was so sharp, it felt like anger. What did this guy have that allowed him into the forbidden world where beings like Olmedo performed for the elite? And with a woman at his side!

Sky kept walking, till he had nearly circled the

block. He looked over a brick wall in the adjoining street and realized he could see the rear of the club, the back door lit by a single bulb. The wall wasn't that high.

If Sky'd been in his right mind, he would never have hoisted himself on top of that wall, avoiding the shards of glass embedded in the top, and dropped down in a crouch on the other side. It did occur to him, there in the darkness, that he was probably an insane person. He could be arrested for trespassing. He imagined his father bailing him out of jail. Or checking him out of the hospital after the bouncer was finished with him. *All right, we'll make this quick,* he thought, trotting across the courtyard to the door. The garbage smell was pretty strong, but he was concentrating on the doorknob. Seized it. Wouldn't turn.

What a surprise! People in New York City lock their doors!

Now what, genius?

He looked around. A fire escape was almost within reach, leading up to the second and third floors.

Oh. Breaking and entering.

Just then he heard voices on the other side of the door. Someone was clattering open the lock. In a panic Sky crouched down behind the trash cans. He was in shadow but not completely hidden, and he tucked his feet tightly against his body as the door opened and two black men stepped out. They were five feet from him.

"Letting up," said one.

The other grunted.

Nothing for half a minute. Then a scratching sound and the smell of a cigarette.

"What's with Art tonight?"

"He's always like that."

"First he bitchin' at you, then he bitchin' at me."

"Ach," said the other voice dismissively.

There was silence for a long time. Sky was getting a cramp in his leg. He wanted fiercely to move it.

"What's the time?" said the same voice.

"We got another five."

Another silence.

"I don't think he looks so good. Do you think he's looking good?"

"Ach."

"I don't think he's looking so good."

Sky was gripping his calf, trying to work the cramp out.

"What do you think? Do you think he's looking good?"

No answer.

"Well . . ." Someone was taking a deep drag. Then a cigarette bounced off the lid of a trash can and landed beside Sky. "What do you say?"

"Let's go."

Sky peered around the edge of the trash can in time to see the door swing shut. On a wild impulse he jumped up and caught it before it slammed. He waited, breathing hard. Seconds passed. Slowly, he pulled the door open and slipped inside.

He started down a dim hallway. *I thought you had plans for your life,* he said inside his head. *Like driving a car someday. Or living long enough to take Suze to the dance.*

A confusion of voices reached him as he poked his head around a bend in the hallway. Ahead stretched the main room of the club, the tables packed, a couple of waiters hurrying to deliver drinks before the next set started. A piano stood under a spotlight on an empty stage beside a drum set and a reclining bass violin.

Suddenly, heavy footsteps were approaching from very nearby. Sky wheeled around. A staircase he hadn't noticed rose to his left—probably to offices, he figured.

There'd been a door halfway down the hall. He ran to it and dove in.

He couldn't see a thing. What he smelled wasn't good.

Footsteps thudded past. Backing up, his shoe hit something that clattered loudly to the floor. After a long while he heard a voice making an announcement of some kind, followed by applause.

Sky cracked open the door. His pulse was running fast. No, it was the distant thrumming of a bass. Then a piano line—no chords at all, just a line of running notes—came in at twice the speed. Finally, the drummer—sticks on cymbals—joined the race. "Hurry Up," it was called. Sky had listened to the thing countless times, but he hadn't a prayer of playing it.

He opened the closet door a fraction wider. Vague light revealed a vacuum cleaner beside him, a mop, rags, and a jar of paint thinner. He didn't dare leave his lair, but he needed to watch Olmedo do the impossible. Glancing around, he padded to the end of the hall. Around the corner, not twenty feet away, sat Art Olmedo in full fling, staring straight at him!

My God! Sky thought, fighting the shocked impulse to flee. Olmedo lifted his head, tilting toward a corner of the ceiling, and his blind eyes drifted closed while the bass and drums stormed along beside him.

It was amazing actually to *see* him, after only hearing him for years. Sky was surprised at how dark he was. He had never thought of Olmedo as white, black, or purple. He was Olmedo. He was also Honduran, Sky knew from reading the album covers. His forehead bulged, as if with an intensity of thought, and every once in awhile he let out a groan, whether of satisfaction or pain, it was impossible to say.

Olmedo followed "Hurry Up" with a traditional ballad, "You Go to My Head," played with quiet reverence, although no one would mistake his spiky chord clusters for the tune's usual harmonies. Sky would happily have settled in there at the bend of the hallway for the rest of the evening; but he happened, just then, to notice the bouncer on the other side of the smoky room looking in his direction. The guy was frowning. He was starting to move.

Sky backed into the shadows, his heart bumping. Time to leave! He trotted down the hall to the back door. A moment later he was outside, the misty rain tickling his face. A quick run across the courtyard, and then he was hoisting himself over the wall. A jag of glass stabbed his hand as he dropped down on the other side and took off. The hand was bleeding, he noticed, but it was more a scrape than a cut. He was appalled to think about the chances he had taken.

Sky walked for some time, not noticing the direction. When finally he looked around, he was surprised to find himself again at the corner of Sixth Avenue and Fourth Street, barely a block from the Turnip. Somehow he'd been walking in a circle—*a circle of rain,* he thought—like a murderer drawn back to the scene of a crime. At that moment, as if on cue, the door to the club opened, and the bouncer leaned out, holding an umbrella for someone. A smaller man, muffled in a cape and hat, stepped outside, tapping the sidewalk gingerly with a white cane.

Sky stood watching as the figure came toward

him, stepping in puddles that he couldn't see. The man held a battered briefcase under one arm, to protect it. Alone at two o'clock in the morning, in frigid rain, the great, blind Art Olmedo was walking home.

Sky didn't move. The man tapped closer, passing within a few feet of him, and kept on his way. Sixth Avenue is very wide at this point, like a bend in a river, and Sky worried how Olmedo was going to get across. The rain-slicked cobblestones didn't make it easier. Sky started to follow him.

That was the moment hell chose to break loose. Olmedo had just stepped from the curb when a sedan roared around the corner, a swerving smear of black. Sky thought the driver may have caught a glimpse of the white cane, because the car swung suddenly in the other direction. But it was too late. The back of the car skidded sideways, knocking Olmedo against an overflowing trash can. The briefcase flew into the air, papers sailing in all directions, while the can rumbled like a kettledrum and came to rest in the gutter. The car roared on, diminishing in the distance.

Sky ran and knelt beside Olmedo, who lay groaning against a No Parking sign.

God, no!

A thin line of blood ran down from the old man's lip. Sky reached out, but then pulled back his hand.

What should he do? He tried to remember the first-aid course he'd taken in summer school two years ago. You weren't supposed to move people with broken bones. Were any bones broken?

"You okay?"

Olmedo opened his sightless eyes and frowned. "Ow," he said.

Sky reached out and grasped him by the arm.

"*OW!*"

Okay, we won't do that, thought Sky. "Stay here," he said, then stood and ran into the middle of the street. It wasn't the best time of night to grab a taxi, or the best weather. While there, he picked up the briefcase and as many pieces of paper as he could find. To his surprise, they were blank, with bumps all over them. *Braille,* he realized. He stuffed them into the satchel and picked up the cane, which had broken almost in two.

Miraculously, a Yellow cab pulled up. Sky opened the door and gestured for the driver to wait, then hurried back to Olmedo.

"Come on. Upsa-daisy!" He reached around the man's waist and tried to lift him. Olmedo growled a bit but was making an effort. Finally, they were standing, the blind man swaying as he held on to the parking sign.

"This way."

"*Mierda!*" Olmedo muttered as Sky guided him to the car.

"Easy."

"Is he drunk?" said the driver, turning around in his seat. "I don't want no drunks messing up my car."

Sky shook his head. "He's hurt."

"Whatcha say?" He looked at the blind man more closely. "Hey," he exclaimed. "He's bleedin'! You takin' him to St. Vincent's?"

Olmedo opened his eyes, spooking the driver with his milky pupils.

"Hey, he's blind!"

Sky nodded.

"No hospital!" said Olmedo, his eyes closing in a wince.

"No hospital. Okay, so where does he want to go?"

Sky turned to Olmedo. "Where do you live?"

The old man wasn't listening. He was too busy muttering curses.

Sky overcame his qualms and reached into Olmedo's coat pocket, extracting a black wallet shiny with wear.

There has to be some I.D., he thought, though it was hard to tell with all the receipts and cards, many of which spilled onto the floor of the cab. He picked them up, along with a small square object he recognized as a condom. Finally, he found what he needed: name, address, apartment number. He showed it to the driver.

"That's two blocks from here," said the cabbie.

"Good. Go on."

The taxi lurched up Sixth Avenue, then made a left onto Washington Place. Sky got out in front of a grim-looking building and helped the groaning Olmedo to his feet. He tossed a couple of dollars into the front seat.

"Naw," said the driver.

Sky looked at him uncomprehendingly.

"You're a good kid." The man poked the money back in Sky's hand. "I like seeing a good kid."

"Thanks."

"Wish I could say the same about my own." The driver gave a little wave and sped off.

Sky looked at Olmedo, who was now leaning against the building. "You got a key?"

But he wasn't helping. Sky reached into Olmedo's pocket and extracted a key ring while the jazzman cursed in Spanish.

Later Sky wondered how he'd ever gotten him upstairs. There was the front door—a wrought-iron monster backed with heavy glass—then the ancient elevator, moaning all the way to the poorly lit sixth floor. Finally, the door to the apartment itself.

Inside, Sky discovered that the ceiling light didn't work. *Why should it?* he realized. *What did this guy need to see?* The light coming in through the window showed a room sparsely furnished, just a chair, a sofa, some sort of hi-fi equipment in the corner, and a shiny piano.

There were two other doors, one to the kitchen, the other to a small bedroom. It was there that Sky guided the musician, gently lowering him onto the bed.

Olmedo winced as Sky pulled off his shoes. *"Ai! Qué hace?"*

Sky looked at him. Having always thought of Art Olmedo as a sort of giant, he was surprised at how small he actually was. *A dark little man,* Sky thought, *in a dark little room.* Carefully, he slid the wallet and key chain back into the man's pocket. Better than putting them on the table, where they might never be found.

Olmedo's feet were cold. Pulling off the wet socks, Sky unfolded a blanket and spread it over him, tucking the bottom under his bony ankles. Before long the sound of breathing deepened, becoming slow and regular.

By the front door Sky paused and looked back, watching the shadows of branches swaying across the floor. They reminded him of branches he'd seen from his own dark living room just a few hours ago. Same night, same city, held in the same shining circle of rain.

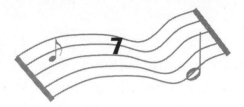

Truscott was in fine form Monday morning, if you like knife-throwing acts. This was the day everybody had to get their topics approved for the paper due Friday. They'd read three Shakespeare plays this semester and could write about any one they wanted. Most kids picked *Romeo and Juliet*. A few of the guys took *Macbeth*. Sky was drawn to *Hamlet*. To everyone's surprise, Truscott seemed to think Sky's idea was not so bad. "Interesting," he called it.

It was the only subject Sky could come up with: How Shakespeare uses music in the play.

"Of course," Truscott said, "you won't find enough on music. You'll want to expand the topic to the performing arts generally. Do you think you can manage that?"

Sky nodded. He had no idea if he could do that or not.

"Then go to it, Mr. Schuyler. Go to it!"

Max punched Sky on the arm when Truscott turned to the blackboard.

After the last class of the day the two friends dawdled down the stairs. Sky slid his heavy briefcase along the banister while Max kept pumping him for details about his run-in with Art Olmedo. He couldn't get enough of it. What did the guy look like? What was his apartment like? What did he say?

"Sorry, I don't know Spanish curse words."

Max shook his head. "Incredible."

As they approached the school's back entrance they discovered the soccer team coagulating around the door. Outside stood a big school bus, grumbling and trembling and generally polluting Ninety-fourth Street. It would carry the players to Central Park for the game with McBurney School. Everybody was excited, because it was the final game of the season and because McBurney's team was even worse than Harmon's. The smell of victory was in the air.

In amongst the boys, bright as marigolds, stood a cluster of cheerleaders, laughing and talking and standing on one leg and fixing their hair and pulling up their gym socks. Sky gave a little wave to Suze, who was untangling her pom-poms. He never thought of her as a cheerleader type. Editor, yes; critic, skeptic, for sure. Laugher at the laughable. But she also had this other side, school loyalty or something. It was kind of a shock to see her in a short skirt, and Sky had a moment of goofball pride to think that this was the girl he was taking to the Winter Dance.

She came over. "Going to the game?"

"Sure!" he blurted. Actually, the plan had been to get in some practicing before Max's mom came home from work.

"How about this other guy?"

Max pushed out his underlip in his "maybe" expression. The farther out the lip, the more doubtful his view. "I guess we could stop by for a while. It being the final game and all."

"Hey," she said gaily, "how often do you get to see Harmon actually win a game?"

"Or you with pom-poms," said Max.

"You know me," she said, "school spirit all the way!"

"Did she really say that?" Max said.

They pushed through the crowd and out to the sidewalk. Sky held the neck of his windbreaker closed as he and Max climbed the street to Columbus Avenue.

"Stop for an egg cream?" said Max, whose jacket was as thin as Sky's. "I got this thing for egg creams."

"Okay."

They arrived at their usual place on the corner of Ninety-sixth and slid onto stools at the counter. Sky sipped a cup of coffee and watched as the soda guy squirted some chocolate syrup in a glass, then filled the glass with fizzy water and gave it a stir.

"One egga crema, comin' up!" He placed it with a flourish in front of Max.

"Why do you like these things?" said Sky. "They

don't have eggs in them and they don't have cream."

"This is true." Max took a swallow and smacked his lips. "I hear you're taking Da Suze to the dance."

"Where'd you hear that?"

"I was going to ask her myself, but she said a little weasel got there first."

"That's me, the little weasel."

Max looked at him. "You're a smug bastard."

"You're jealous."

"Damn straight." Max drained his egg cream. "You want to double? I'm thinking of asking Jill."

"Jill Coverton?"

"What's wrong with that?"

"She's nice."

"Yes, she is."

"Why would she go with you?"

"Ha-ha."

They paid, then looked through the magazine rack, but found nothing racier than *Popular Mechanics.* The double-date idea sounded good to Sky. It took the pressure off. Of course, he thought as they stepped outside and headed toward the park, it was also a way for Max to go out with Suze without seeming to— without even buying the corsage.

He glanced over. Max was kicking a bottle cap ahead of him on the sidewalk. He passed it over to Sky, who passed it back.

By the time they reached the field, the game was under way, though it was hard to tell what was going on. Most of the players were scurrying around at the far end. The six Harmon cheerleaders huddled to keep warm.

"There's Jill," said Max, heading over to the girls.

"You going to ask her?"

"Watch and learn."

Sky had to admire the way his friend could just walk up to a bunch of girls—girls in short skirts yet—and start a conversation. Jill, he noticed, was a perfectly fine-looking person, with friendly, somewhat heavy-lidded eyes and dark blond hair. She looked good in goose bumps.

Sky ambled closer. He remembered the long-ago night a bunch of kids had ended up at Jill's place after a late basketball game. Her mother had been there, he recalled, a large shy woman who'd served everyone squares of homemade pizza. Sky had never run into anchovies before and vowed never to let it happen again.

Yes, Jill was all right.

Right now she was laughing. Suze came over and joined in.

"So we're on?" Max was saying.

"Sure, okay." Jill looked up and saw Sky. "Hey," she said.

"Hey."

"I think we're double-dating. Is that okay?"

Before he could answer, the players stampeded up the field and a muddy soccer ball hurtled over the heads of bystanders. Sky ran after it and flung it to the waiting forward, who happened to be Steve Glass, flecked with sweat and bleeding from his knee. Glass plunged back into the game without a word.

Minutes later a foul was called against McBurney, and the cheerleaders, who'd been looking for an excuse, burst onto the field.

"Harmon, Harmon, red and *gold*!" they shouted, "Old McBurney's going to *fold*!"

Six yellow sweaters, six bright red H's. The girls were smiling, except Suze, who was actually laughing—at herself, Sky suspected.

"Harmon, Harmon, gold and *red*!"

Sky was waiting for the jump. Boys always wait for the jump.

"Send McBurney back to *bed*! Yeeaaay team!!"

Up they went. All six of them. Two in particular.

Sky turned, smiling, and noticed Truscott in a dark overcoat standing apart from the others. He'd been watching the school cheer, but he didn't smile or clap. His face, in fact, had a pensive look, and it occurred to Sky that he had as few friends among the faculty as he had among the students.

The girls came back to the sidelines giggling, breathing hard. Max gave Sky a nudge. "Got something to write on? I need to get Jill's number."

"Sure." He patted his clothes. In his shirt pocket he felt something flat and square. It was a blank card with a number of small bumps on it. "Omigod!"

"What?"

"Must have been when I dropped his wallet in the taxi."

"Is that Olmedo's?" Max took the card and turned it around.

"I better get it back to him."

"When?"

"I don't know. Now, I guess."

"Want me to come?"

Sky considered it. "I guess not. I'll just—"

Jill looked from one to the other in friendly bewilderment.

Max took the card and showed it to her. Suze peered over his shoulder. "See this card?" he said. "See what it says?"

"It doesn't say anything," said Jill.

"That's where you're wrong." He handed it back to Sky. "Call me tonight, okay?"

Sky nodded.

"Bye," said Jill. She raked her fingers through her long hair.

"See ya, big guy," said Suze.

Sky hurried to Central Park West to catch a downtown subway. His father would expect him home to make dinner, so there wasn't a lot of time. Waiting for the train, he stared at the card, half expecting a message to materialize. He didn't want to go. Olmedo would have no idea who he was. He probably wasn't even home.

Twenty minutes later Sky was cutting across Washington Square as the last sunlight gleamed on the square-topped tower of Judson Church. He knew about that place. It was a cultural mecca of the Village, home of jazz concerts and beatnik poetry readings. Not that Sky had been to any.

Another couple of minutes brought him to the building where Olmedo lived. It looked less grim in daylight but just as grimy.

Pulling open the heavy glass door, he found himself before a row of buzzers and tarnished mailboxes. There was the name, below a white button.

He gave the button a push. No response. He waited with growing relief.

Well, we tried. He gave the button one more push and turned to go.

"Diga!" The Hispanic syllables came through a blast of static.

"Mr. Olmedo? Hello, my name's Alec Schuyler, and I've got—"

"Who is this?"

"My name—"

"Can't hear you."

The line went dead. Sky's stomach felt hollow. Should he push the button again? There were no slits in the mailboxes, or he would have wedged the card in and called it a day.

He pushed the button.

Another blast of static. "Go away!"

As he stood uncertainly, the outside door opened, and a woman of about sixty came in with a bag of groceries from Gristede's. She threw him a look as she got out her key. He watched her deciding whether he was going to mug her or not.

Apparently, he passed.

"Thanks," he said, following her in.

"You're seeing who?"

He held the elevator door. "Mr. Olmedo?"

She shook her head. The elevator groaned and clanked. She looked at Sky again. "You a friend of his?"

"No."

"What?"

"No!"

"Didn't think so." The door opened on five and she held it with her backside. "Tell him," she said, "Mrs. Kepper don't appreciate him playing at two o'clock in the morning." She stepped off and let the metal gate crash behind her.

Sky took the elevator to six. Three apartment doors stood catty-corner, with no name on any of them, but Sky remembered Olmedo's and knocked loudly.

So what's he going to do? Shoot me?

"Who is it?" came an irritated voice.

"I've got something of yours, Mr. Olmedo."

"I told you to go away."

"It's something in Braille. I can't read it."

"Put it under the door."

"Can't you open the door a minute?"

"No."

Sky didn't know why it was important to get this disagreeable man to open the door. It wasn't as though he was going to *see* Sky; but it was incomplete this way. It was . . . rude.

"I'm the guy who took you home the other night."

"What?"

"I got you home."

A pause. He heard the cluck of the dead bolt, then the clink of the door chain, and finally the metallic groan of the Fox lock, the very latest in security devices.

The door opened three inches, revealing one eye, milky; one bulging forehead, brown; and one unshaven cheek. "Tall for a kid, aren't ya?"

Sky was flummoxed by the question. "A little," he said.

"Well, don't just stand there in your funky little windbreaker, come in." Olmedo opened the door wide, and Sky saw that his left arm was held in a sling. The man turned and walked stiffly to a black leather chair, then sat down and stretched his skinny legs before him, crossing them at the ankles. In his dungarees and gray T-shirt he could have been the building's super. Sky looked at him closely. Kind of an ugly cuss. No wonder he didn't put his picture on his albums.

"What you staring at? Never seen a blind guy before?"

"How—?"

"Speak, for godsake!"

"How do you know I'm staring?"

"I can *hear* you staring."

Sky was silent. He pulled out the card from his shirt pocket. "Here. This is yours."

Olmedo reached out his good arm. He felt the card, looking up at the ceiling as he did so. Then he laughed. It was a short laugh, not much more than a bark, but it briefly transformed his face. "What are you doing with my girlfriend's number?"

"I didn't—"

"You ain't ready for her. How old are you? Fourteen?"

"Fifteen."

"You hurt my arm, you know."

Sky stared at the sling.

"When you tried to get me up," the man went on. "Other than that, you did good."

Sky was silent.

"You didn't break it, just pulled it out a little."

"Sorry."

"No big deal. Keeps my mind off my ribs."

The two of them sat without speaking for most of a minute. "Man of few words," he said at last.

Sky didn't know what to say.

"Want a beer or something?"

"No thanks."

"You want something. What is it?"

Sky had not been aware that he wanted anything.

"Money?" Olmedo said.

"No."

"I suppose I owe you."

"No!"

"What, then?"

"Nothing."

"Don't lie."

Sky looked down. "Well," he said. He knew how odd this would sound. "Could you show me the last chords—the last *two* chords—of 'Regeneration'?"

"What!" Olmedo sat up straight.

"I just can't figure them out."

Olmedo was silent a long time. Between the two of them, they could generate a lot of dead air. "I don't want to show you that," he said.

"Oh."

"Anything else?"

"I guess not."

Silence.

"So you play, then."

"I guess."

"You guess. So you *think* you play, but you're not sure."

"I play."

"That's better. So play."

"What?"

"Sit your ass down and play me something! God, the kid's deaf!"

This was awful. Sky was not going to play in front of Art Olmedo.

"Play or get out. You're wasting my time."

Sky went to the baby grand. It was kind of beat-up, now that he looked at it, with drink rings and even a cigarette mark or two, but it was a Steinway. He'd never played on such an instrument. He slid onto the bench, his mind racing over the pieces he knew.

Sky's heart was beating hard, and he knew that was going to affect his hands. *Keep to something slow,* he decided.

He launched into "'Round Midnight," the soulful Thelonious Monk tune with the slow descending bass line. All the while, he struggled to put out of his mind the person sitting in the chair behind him, but it was like playing with a tiger in the room. He got through the piece clumsily, his fingers thick on the keys.

Olmedo was silent. Sky turned to look at him. The guy was going through a bunch of Braille cards. He was fingering them, then setting them in two little piles. Had he been listening at *all*?

"Play me a chord," said Olmedo finally. "Any chord."

Sky played a C-seventh with a D major laid an octave above it. He always thought it had a jazzy sound.

"Now play it loud."

Sky hit it again, with more force.

"Louder!"

Sky hit it as hard as he knew how.

"Play it louder!"

"I can't!"

"Play it louder or get the hell out of here!"

Sky pounced on the chord with such force that the piano shuddered forward on its casters.

"Thank you." Olmedo continued sorting his cards.

Sky stared at him, furious.

Finally, Olmedo laid his hands on top of the Braille cards and looked up. "Somebody doesn't want you playing the piano. Am I right?"

Sky's eyes widened.

"What I want to know," the man went on, "is it you, or is it somebody else?"

"I guess it's my father."

"Do you guess it's your father?"

"It's my father."

"Good, because if it was you, I'd tell you to get out of here. I'm not a shrink."

"What made you—?"

"Do you realize you played that entire Monk tune with the soft pedal down?"

"I did?"

"Like you wanted to play it, but you didn't want me to hear it."

Sky took that in.

"What would he do," said Olmedo, "if you played regular? You know, loud and soft. Like a person. Would he beat you up?"

"Oh, no!"

"Would he yell at you?"

"Actually," said Sky, his voice even quieter than usual, "he got rid of the piano a couple months ago."

"*What!*" Olmedo jumped up. He looked like he

was about to hit Sky. Instead, he moved to the windowsill and picked up a pack of Lucky Strikes. He seemed to be trying to control himself. "So what do you play on?" he said.

"Sometimes I go to a friend's house. He's got a little piano."

"Did anybody ever tell you you need to speak up?"

"A *friend.* He's got a little *piano.*"

"How little?" He lit a cigarette and shook the match.

"Four octaves."

"Four whole octaves!"

Neither spoke for a while.

"Well, you can't practice here!" Olmedo burst out.

"Oh, I know that!"

"And just so you know, I don't take students. I stopped teaching a long time ago."

"I heard."

"So if you were thinking about that . . ."

"No, no."

Olmedo paced, but he always managed to reach the ashtray on the windowsill before the ash fell off the end of his cigarette. It was like he was psychic. Finally, he stubbed it out. "I'll put in a call to the guy who runs Judson. You know the Judson Church?"

"Sure!"

"They got a shit piano, but it's got more than four octaves."

"Thanks!"

"All right, good." Olmedo kept circling. "You want a suggestion? Maybe you don't want a suggestion."

"I do. Of course!"

"Stay away from Monk for a while. Cats who play a lot of Monk start sounding like him. Monkeys, I call them. You want to sound like—what's your name?"

"Sky."

"Right. You want to sound like Sky. You can go back to Monk later."

"I see."

"Just an idea."

"Yes. I see."

Olmedo kept pacing. It amazed Sky that he didn't bump into anything. Maybe that was why he had so little furniture.

"You practice scales?" said Olmedo suddenly.

"Some. Not a lot."

"How did I know?"

"Should I do more scales?"

Olmedo leaned back against the windowsill and folded his arms. "You should do *only* scales. Scales and chords. Of course, you don't know any chords."

Okay, thought Sky, *the jazz master of the world is telling me that I don't have talent.*

"You know some Monk chords. You know some Olmedo chords. Almost."

Sky swallowed. "Could you show——?"

"I don't teach."

Sky sighed.

"Anyway, it's too soon to think about that. You gotta hear before you can play."

"Hear what?"

"Something that won't influence you. Like Lester Young on tenor sax. You got any Lester?"

"I think so. Playing with the Basie band."

"Go home. Listen to his solo. Any solo."

"Okay."

"Listen until you know it by heart."

"Okay."

"Then come back here and sing it for me."

"Sing?"

"Yes, I want you to come back here and sing it for me. I can see you Thursday, this same time." He pushed himself away from the sill. "Now, if you don't mind . . ."

Sky stood uncertainly. "Could I ask one more question?"

"Quick."

"How'd you know I was wearing a windbreaker?"

Olmedo frowned. "Listen sometime. You know that slippery material they use? It makes a racket."

"Oh."

"Now, I'd appreciate it if you'd get out of here. I got work to do."

8

Sky had the onions sizzling and was starting to slice last night's baked potato into them when his father came downstairs.

"Smells good," said Quinn, rubbing his hands.

"Home fries okay?"

"Great."

"Thought I'd make an omelette."

"That's perfect." His father opened the fridge and got himself a pickle. "How come you're late?"

"Soccer game." Sky was learning how to lie without actually lying. He knew he wasn't very good at it.

"You don't play soccer."

"I was watching."

"School spirit, eh?" Quinn crunched the pickle in half. "Since when?"

Sky was suddenly wary. His father was a whiz at questioning.

"I don't know." He lit the oven with a match, waiting for the soft explosion, then put in the cherry pie he'd picked up at the bakery.

"You probably went to Max Whatsisface to practice the piano."

"Actually, I didn't." Lie without lying.

"So who was the other team?"

"McBurney."

"They any good?"

"Lousy." Sky shook the heavy iron frying pan and set it down again. The potatoes were getting golden around the edges.

"So you won, then?"

Watch out. Don't make up anything. He watched his father run his hand over his round head. Always a sign.

"Um."

"Did you win or did you lose? Not a hard question."

"I don't know."

"How could you not know?"

"I didn't stay."

Quinn Schuyler poured himself a big glass of milk and took a gulp. "You didn't stay."

"Not the whole time. You want scrambled?"

"Where'd you go?"

"I don't know. Home."

"Home? You mean the game's still going on at seven o'clock in the pitch dark?"

"No, no." Sky stared at the frying pan.

"Such a simple thing. Why are you lying to me?"

"I'm not lying. I'm cooking."

"Where did you *go?*" There went the hand again over his bald head.

"Dad, can you just tell me? Do you want scrambled?"

Quinn's fist came down on the table. "Damn the damn eggs!"

Sky was silent. The potatoes were about to burn. He took them off the flame. "Actually," he said slowly.

"What?"

"We were talking to a couple of girls."

Quinn looked up sharply.

"That's why we went to the game."

"That's why who went?"

"Me and Max."

"Ah."

"Max wanted to ask one of them to the Winter Dance."

"One of what?"

"The *cheerleaders*, Dad!"

"Oh." A strange little smile played around his father's mouth. "And did he ask?"

"He did."

"And is she going, this cheerleader?"

"She is. In fact, we're double-dating."

His father, who had lifted the glass of milk, set it down again. "*You* have a date?"

"Of course."

His father obviously hadn't thought of Sky in this

way. "So who is this date? Another cheerleader?"

Sky had to smile. "Dad, cheerleading is the least of—"

"*You're* dating a cheerleader?"

"Well, yeah, sure."

"My son, the man of mystery! How come you didn't tell me this in the first place?"

Sky shrugged.

Quinn was smiling broadly. He came over, laid a heavy hand on his son's shoulder, and gave him a shake. "Good for you!"

Sky started the eggs.

Twenty minutes later Quinn was deeply into his second slice of pie. *Is this a man worried about a heart condition?* Sky thought. He noticed his father's ears moved when he chewed. Maybe everybody's did, but without hair it was noticeable. He averted his eyes. The phone rang.

"Are you here?" said Sky, reaching for it.

"If it's Gina Lollobrigida, I'm in."

"Hello?"

"Sky?"

His heart lifted with the upward lilt of the voice. It was just automatic. "Suze! Hey."

"Hey. You got a minute?"

"Sure, sure." He looked over at his father.

Quinn's eyes widened. "This is the one?"

Sky said a silent "Sh."

His father stuck out his lower lip. "Ah so."

"Can you hold a sec, Suze? Maybe I can change phones."

"No, no!" stage-whispered Quinn, struggling from the table. "I'm just leaving." As he passed the boy he gave him a thumbs-up.

Sky closed his eyes. "Yeah," he said when his father was gone. "I'm here."

"I don't know, Sky," came Suze's voice, cool and light, "I didn't know who to talk to. Max would tell me what to do, but I don't think I want him to. You never tell me what to do."

Sky had to laugh. "That's because I don't know anything."

"You know a lot. You just don't say a lot."

He didn't answer. Suze had called him maybe twice in his entire life, and both times were about the band.

"See?" There was a giggle in her voice, a nervous one. "There you go not saying anything."

"Suze, is something wrong?"

"Yes. No. I don't know."

Sky waited.

"I think I want to quit the magazine."

"Oh no." He said it quietly, but some things you don't have to say out loud.

"I know. It was so perfect."

"You can't. You love it."

"I do. I really, really do."

He waited. She would tell him more if she wanted.

"Maybe I'm imagining things. Do you think I'm imagining things?"

"Are you getting a lot of flak?"

"Sure. Oh, yeah. Three girlfriends at least have been snubbing me in the hall. And forget about the upper-classmen. Except the ones who've started hitting on me. Like now, suddenly, it's all right. You don't mind me telling you this, do you?"

"'Course not."

"But we expected that," she went on. "Like you said at lunch that time, they're already jealous."

"Then what is it?"

Five seconds would be a long pause for Suze. She let ten go by. Then, unexpectedly, she laughed. "You know? I can't tell you. Because I'm probably wrong."

"Suze, what is it?"

"No, no, it's stupid."

"It's Truscott, isn't it?"

"Yes."

"My God."

"It's not like he's tried anything. He's been a perfect gentleman."

Sky tried to imagine Truscott as a perfect gentleman.

"Really," she added quickly, "I have no reason to say what I said. It's just that I catch him looking at me sometimes."

Sky was thinking, *Who wouldn't look at the Suze?*

"And he can get awfully close sometimes, when we're going over manuscripts."

"How close?"

"I could tell you what aftershave he uses."

"No thanks."

"Exactly."

"What will you do?"

"I don't know. What if I'm wrong? I can't tell you how I like this editing job. It's not an ego thing, it's just that I've finally found something I'm good at."

Was there anything she wasn't good at?

"Could you do me a huge, big favor?"

"Sure."

"Could you apply for the *Harmon Review* staff and come to meetings and tell me what you think?"

She was right. It was a huge favor. "Sure."

"Sky, you're the best."

He laughed.

"Okay," she said, "so I won't quit until I get your take on it."

"Okay."

"Okay, well, thanks."

"Okay."

"See you tomorrow?"

Sky nodded and hung up the phone.

As it happened, there were two pianos at Judson Church, one in the basement community room and one in the choir loft. The basement was being used, so the young custodian pointed out the stairs to the loft. Sky had been inside a church maybe half a dozen times in his life. Quinn Schuyler was contemptuous of formal religion, so after a few tries early in their marriage his wife had given up. It was that or give up on the marriage, and by then she had a baby on the way. Sky had learned about this during the last month of his mother's life, when she'd asked him to bring her a box from the bottom of her dresser. It contained a rosary.

When he reached the loft, Sky went immediately to the piano, a sturdy old upright bearing the scars of hard use. He played a chord. Not a bad sound. A little echoey. He stood and looked out over the expanse of the sanctuary, lined by tall stained-glass windows.

Mine, all mine. Until six o'clock.

He sat down and noodled out a blues, then stopped midway. His left foot, he realized, had been holding down the soft pedal.

But could he play at full volume? Wouldn't it bother people?

What people?

He padded downstairs. It took him awhile to find the custodian. "Look," he said, "I don't want to bother people by playing too loud."

The custodian was in his early twenties maybe, with caramel skin, a pencil-line mustache, and a handsome smile. A pair of sunglasses perched atop his carefully disheveled black hair. "Hey," he said, giving the top of his turtleneck a little tug, "Olmedo said to take care of you. Play as loud as you want."

"And the people down in the meeting room?"

"Can't hear a thing."

Sky smiled as he climbed back to the loft. *All mine.* An hour and a half later, his hands tingling after a workout on some Gerry Mulligan tunes and a solid half hour of scales, Sky reluctantly closed the piano. He had to get home early enough for his father to believe he'd been studying at the Seventy-ninth Street branch of the New York Public. That meant he actually had to *go* to the library and grab a book.

"Hey," said the custodian as Sky was leaving, "you don't sound so bad."

"Thanks, man."

"Name's Federico. Friends call me Rico."

They shook hands. "I'm Sky."

Federico nodded and pushed open the heavy door. "Catch you later."

Sky gave a little wave, then hurried across the street

into Washington Square, his jacket ballooning in the wind as he zipped it closed. *If I could somehow make this a regular thing . . . ,* he thought, a giggle of hope climbing his throat.

He noticed a trio of pigeons flapping from the top of the great arch at the north end of the park. They swerved overhead in formation, like a triad chord changing from major to minor and back, finally fluttering to the ground in front of a man sitting on a bench with his legs stretched before him and a long white cane propped by his side.

Sky stopped, amazed to see the man he'd been thinking about all afternoon. Olmedo reached in the pocket of his dark coat and pulled out a handful of crumbs, scattering them before him. More pigeons arrived, strutting and pecking. Occasionally, one would flap into the air, then settle. He tossed another handful but seemed inattentive.

Of course he would come here. He lived just a couple of blocks away. It occurred to Sky to go up and thank him for making the call to Judson, but somehow he couldn't do it. It was like there was a wall of silence around the man. Instead, Sky slipped onto an empty bench across the walkway. They sat without speaking, two figures, one white and fifteen, one dark and sixty, separated by a dozen excited pigeons.

Sky felt guilty sitting there, but he kept watching as

if he could learn something, as if there were a secret. All he came up with was how ordinary Olmedo looked. You wouldn't glance at him twice. One of the great jazz players of his time looked like a nobody.

Which made two of them.

What is he thinking about? Sky wondered. *What does he want? What does he really want?*

I'll never know.

He got up quietly, careful not to scuffle his shoes in the leaves, and headed east toward the subway, leaving Olmedo to the birds and his thoughts.

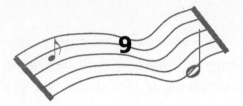

9

"**Y**ou said you were going to the library."

"I did."

"No, you didn't. I called and had them page you."

"You called?"

"Twice."

"But why?"

"To be sure you were telling the truth."

So there it was: Quinn Schuyler thought his son was a liar. Sky pulled a heavy library book from his briefcase and thumped it on the kitchen table.

"I must have been in the stacks. I didn't hear you."

Quinn hefted the book. *"Shakespeare's Imagery and What It Tells Us.* Well, well."

"Believe me now?"

Quinn handed it back without comment.

Sky should have been elated—he was learning to be a good liar after all—but instead, he felt depressed. It had come to distrust on his father's side, anger on his. After a silent dinner of hamburgers, coleslaw, and Dave Rubin's pickles, Sky remained in the kitchen to handle the dishes and make a start on his homework. As it happened, the volume he'd laid his hands on at the library was more helpful than he'd expected. A fat old tome, it cataloged the images used in many Shakespeare plays, including the music and theater references in *Hamlet*. There was the play-within-a-play, the talk of "sweet bells jangled," mentions of trumpets and "keeping time," and the wonderful: "'Sblood, do you think that I am easier to be played on than a pipe?'"

This Hamlet cat was mysterious. He could be likable and offensive in the space of a breath. A man of action who didn't act. Until he did.

He wasn't the only mystery in Sky's life. Who could make sense of Truscott? Or Olmedo? The words of Sky's mother came back to him: "We never know enough to judge another person." She had said that about Sky's father. She was lying in bed three weeks before her death.

But it's so hard *not* to judge. Like when your father's ears move when he eats. Or when your teacher starts putting the moves on your friend.

You don't know that.

You don't know enough.

Sky would go to those *Harmon Review* meetings and keep an eye on this guy. He'd watch him like Hamlet watched King Claudius. That was a pretty neat scene,

Sky had to admit, where Hamlet spies on the king at his prayers. What did Truscott pray for?

The magazine staff met during afternoon study hall, but it was pure business—how to share proof-reading chores and who should call local businesses for ads. Truscott didn't show up until near the end of the hour. He stared at Sky like he was seeing Hamlet's ghost. "Well, well," was all he said.

"I asked Sky to join us," said Suze. "He'll be con-tributing some music reviews."

"Aren't we a literary magazine?"

She shrugged prettily. "I thought we could use some variety. We might get a bigger audience."

"You're the editor, dear. By the way, could I see you for a moment after the meeting?"

"Sure, Mr. Truscott."

He swerved out of the room.

Paul Friedman, the layout guy, sniggered: "Can I get you a cup of water, dear?"

Andrea Patchnok simpered, "Can I polish your shoes, dear?"

"Okay, okay," said Suze, blushing.

During sixth-period break Sky loitered in the courtyard with Max, who was showing him a new book of poetry he'd picked up, something called *Howl*, by the Beat poet Allen Ginsberg.

"Listen to this stuff!" Max started reading aloud: "'I saw the best minds of my generation destroyed by madness, starving hysterical naked . . .'"

"Wow," said Sky, who was only half listening. He was thinking he didn't want to see the best girl of his generation destroyed by Truscott. He rubbed the arms of his bulky blue sweater as the breeze picked up.

"'. . . dragging themselves through the negro streets at dawn looking for an angry fix . . .'"

Jill Coverton materialized before them. She didn't look chilly at all. "Whatcha got?"

"Oh, some dirty poetry," said Max.

"Oh boy."

"You're too young."

"Gimme, gimme."

Sky caught sight of Suze standing by the door. Her arms were folded in front of her. "He wants me to have dinner with him tomorrow," she said as he came up to her.

"Isn't he married?" Sky said.

"You get right to the point, don't you?"

"Well, isn't he?"

"I guess. He says he wants to brainstorm with me about the direction of the magazine."

Sky didn't answer.

"He says there isn't enough time during school, which in a way is true."

He bit his underlip.

"I panicked, okay?"

"You mean you said *yes*?"

"I said . . ." She gave a short laugh. "I said that the band had a gig and I had to be there—as the business manager."

"That's funny!" Sky turned clear around in a little circle.

"Why?"

"Because I told my dad I was going out tomorrow with you!"

She recovered quickly. "Why am I always the last to know?"

"It was the only way I could get down to Judson with Max and have a real practice."

Her laugh was pure Suze, starting high and spiking higher.

"I said there was this church function down there," he said, "a party or something, and you asked me to go."

"Oh God, Sky."

"Yeah." They stood silently. "So . . ."

"What?"

"Do you want to make me honest and come along?"

"Why not?"

This was the most amazing luck. Sky always had luck, but it was usually bad.

"Don't forget," she said with a crinkly smile, "it'll make *me* honest too."

"But he'll just ask you again the next day."

"Maybe."

"If he's the kind of guy I think he is."

She was quiet a moment. "I guess I'll have to take my honesty one day at a time."

Sky reached home that afternoon determined to polish off the Shakespeare paper and his geometry so that tomorrow night would be clear. He hadn't counted on finding his father racing around in undershorts with an upraised broom, trying to hit a pigeon. The bird had gotten in through the skylight and was zooming from hallway to bedroom and back. It missed Sky's head by an inch.

"Stand still, you bastard!" yelled Quinn, puffing down the stairs after the frantic bird. The broom knocked a framed photo off the wall.

"Don't hurt him!" said Sky, picking up the picture. It was of himself in fourth grade in a baseball uniform. He was holding a bat and pretending to look at the pitcher, although he was only looking at the photographer.

"He's filthy! He'll give us diseases!"

"Dad, no!"

Whap! Another miss.

The bird flew up the stairway and crashed into the skylight. It fluttered lower, dazed, then sailed into Sky's room at the back of the house. Quinn chugged up the stairs, gasping. "Get him!"

"Dad, he's only trying to get out!" Sky ran to the front room and opened both windows wide. Then he pushed up the skylight with a pole and propped it.

Whap! Whap!

Suddenly, the bird soared over Sky's head, into Quinn's bedroom, and straight out the window.

Sky closed his eyes, holding his forehead on a tripod of fingers. "Thank God," he whispered. He'd begun setting the skylight back in place when his father came into the hallway. His face was flushed, and he leaned against the wall. Below the belly his skinny legs poked out. They looked almost frail, their whiteness contrasting with his tanned face.

"The . . . the . . ."

"Dad!"

Quinn gestured weakly, as if waving to a distant acquaintance.

The medicine! Sky realized, and ran to get it. The container was right in the drawer. He fought open the top.

"Water," he said to himself. He raced to the bathroom for a paper cup and came out to find his father leaning with his back to the wall, still breathing hard.

Quinn downed the pills with a gulp of water and nodded.

"Come on, let's get you into the room." Sky let his father lean against him, surprised at how heavy he was. He helped him onto the bed and eased off his shoes. This was the second time in a week that he'd taken off a man's shoes.

"Should I call Stephens?"

"Never mind."

"I'm going to."

Quinn shook his head, but Sky made the call anyway.

It was reassuring to hear Stephens' warm baritone. "Put him on," the doctor said.

Sky handed over the phone.

"Yes. . . . No. No, nothing like that. . . . Okay. . . . No. I was chasing a damn bird. . . . That's right, a bird!"

Not the most enlightening conversation.

"Here," said Quinn. "He wants to talk to you."

"You did the right thing, Sky," said Stephens. "Just make him rest. No arguments. Let the medicine do its work."

"He's not having . . . ?"

"Doesn't sound like a heart attack, from what I could get out of him, but we'll want to keep an eye on it. You've got my home phone, don't you?"

"Yeah."

"Be sure to use it. I want to know of any change."

"Yes, okay."

"Good boy."

Sky hung up and watched his father's eyes begin to close.

The phone rang again.

Sky grabbed it. "Dr. Stephens?"

"This is Bob Matheson. Is your father there?"

Oh my God, Suze's father! "Could I, um, take a message?"

"Who is it?" said Quinn.

"Is he there or not?" said the voice.

"Dad?" said Sky. "It's for you."

Quinn Schuyler frowned. "Hello?"

Sky hurried to the living room, where he carefully lifted the receiver.

"Glad to hear it." It was Mr. Matheson's voice. "He sounds all right."

"He's a good boy."

"I appreciate that. There are all these beatniks these days."

"I know, I know. A lot of trash out there."

"Can't be too careful."

"Right." Quinn sounded tired. Sky could tell he wanted to get off.

"There's some Jewish kid Susan's been hanging around with lately. You know anything about that?"

"Afraid not."

"Not that there's anything wrong . . ."

"I agree. Absolutely."

"I got some working for me. Fine workers."

"Right, right."

"It's just Susan. She's, well, you know . . ."

"I know."

"She's special."

"Oh, I know. Alec thinks the world of her."

"That so?"

"Always talking about her."

"Really! What does he say?"

"Ohhh . . ."

"No, really. I'm interested."

"Well, that she's special. Really special."

"Well, he's right."

"Great talking to you. I gotta—"

"You happen to know where they're going tomorrow night?"

"He said something about a church function, somewhere downtown."

"Church!"

"That's what he said. Downtown."

"Well! That's fine!"

Sky gently replaced the receiver. His hand was trembling.

♪

Thursday went by in a blur. Finally, the bell rang, and the kids surged out, free till tomorrow. Sky took the Broadway subway to the Village. He had to face Art Olmedo and was dreading it. He was certainly not planning to *sing* for the guy, but he'd keep his word and show up. Maybe he could get him to demonstrate a chord or two.

Sky was puzzled, then, to get no answer at the downstairs bell. He rang several times, with growing disappointment. If the guy was in, he obviously didn't want visitors.

"Looking for Art?"

Sky whirled around to see a large black man with a tiny mustache.

"Um."

"If you goin' up, bring this to 'im." He handed Sky a small paper bag, stapled closed, from a pharmacy. "I don't think he's lookin' so good."

"He didn't answer the bell."

"Right. He's not so good today. That's how come he give me the keys." He jingled them, then dropped them in Sky's hand. "Tell him Manny had to run."

Sky watched him head down the street. *Of course!* he realized. He was one of the guys at the Red Turnip that night, smoking out back.

Sky took the elevator to six and knocked on the

apartment door. There was no answer, so he rang the bell. Then he knocked again. Finally, he remembered the keys. "Hello?" He poked his head inside the apartment. The living room was dark, and a disagreeable smell hung in the air. A trace of vomit.

"Mr. Olmedo?"

He found him in the bedroom, dressed, lying on top of the covers. The sling lay on the night table.

"It's me. Sky."

The man coughed. "Who?"

"Alec Schuyler. You said—"

"Go away."

"I've got your medicine."

Silence. "Where's Manny?"

"He had to go. Here, you want your medicine?"

He took the paper bag. "Get me a glass of water."

Sky hurried to the kitchen. In the cupboard he found, not glasses, but empty jelly jars and filled one with water from the tap. By now Olmedo was sitting up on the bed unscrewing the container of pills. Manny was right: He didn't look so good. He reached out for the water and frowned as he swallowed.

"Who did you say you are?"

"My name's Sky. I came by a few days ago."

"Ah," he said, still getting his bearings. Then he said, "No windbreaker today."

"Just a sweater."

He nodded, his eyes closed. "Next time don't sneak up on me."

"You didn't hear me knocking and ringing the bell?"

"I don't mean today."

Sky shook his head, confused.

"I mean in the park."

Sky's stomach dropped. "I didn't mean . . ."

Olmedo swung his legs off the bed. He seemed to be gathering his forces before attempting to stand.

"I'd just come from Judson Church," said Sky, "and I saw you sitting there . . ."

"It's all right."

"I mean, I wasn't spying or anything."

"It's all right, kid."

"But how did you—? Are you sure you can't see?"

"Am I sure?"

"I mean, can you see?"

"I can't see shit. I can hear." He got to his feet and walked slowly to the black leather chair in the living room.

"But I didn't make any noise."

"Uh-huh." He sank into the chair with a sigh.

"Did I?"

"Your windbreaker did. So are you going to sing for me or not?"

"I—"

"Sing or get out." He stretched his legs out before him.

"I don't think I can. I mean—"

"Good-bye."

"No, I mean—"

"Pull the door tight. I hate when people don't pull the door all the way. Then I got to get up."

"I'll sing."

"Are you sure?"

"I'm sure."

"Because if you're not sure—"

"I'm sure!"

"Whatcha got?"

"'Pound Cake'?"

"Good."

Sky stood by the piano and tried singing Lester Young's sax solo from "Pound Cake." Partway through, his throat began aching. It got worse as he went on. It felt like fingers were squeezing his windpipe.

Olmedo was silent a long time. "Well," he said finally, "you got the notes."

Somehow Sky knew this wasn't high praise.

"One thing about Prez," said Olmedo, using the nickname that Billie Holliday had given Lester Young, "he played with confidence."

Sky looked down at his feet.

"Do it again."

Sky nodded like the condemned man he was. He launched once more into Prez's solo. His throat still hurt. Maybe a little less.

"Better. One more time. But louder."

Sky sang the sax solo again, this time more audibly, with a hint of Prez's sharpness of attack.

"Yeah!" said Olmedo. "How about scales? Do any?"

Sky sat at the piano and ran through scales in several keys.

Olmedo held up his hand. "Wait! Fingering's all wrong."

Sky held himself back from asking how in the world Olmedo would know what fingering he was using. Anyway, he happened to know that his fingering was correct. Five years of classical lessons had at least taught him that!

"Don't argue with me!" said Olmedo.

"I didn't say a word."

"It's the way you didn't say it. I'm telling you something. The fingering's fine for Mozart, but it won't help you with Monk or Mulligan. Jazz chops are different. You gotta have access to any finger at any time." He sighed. "I can see we got to start at zero here. Play me the scale again, right hand only. This time use only the thumb and third finger."

Sky found it extremely awkward walking up and down the keyboard using only two fingers.

"That was terrible. Now do it again and use the second and third fingers."

That was even more awkward. He kept tripping.

"Okay, come back next week and do it again, this time with the chromatic scale. And learn another solo by Prez."

"Next week?"

"You really got a problem with hearing, don't you?"

"No."

"Okay." Olmedo grasped the arms of his chair, preparing to heave himself up. "You leave me no choice. Come on. We're going out."

"Outside?"

"There you go again. Of course outside. I'm going to teach you to hear."

"Um," said Sky, "do you want me to get your sling?"

"No, but you can help me with my coat."

Sky held an old army jacket for him. Then Olmedo grabbed a white cane—one of several—from behind the door, and they started down. On the street Sky rubbed his arms, a little envious of the jacket. They stopped at the corner of Sixth.

"Red light," said Olmedo.

Sky looked up. "How did you know?"

"Listen."

"To what?"

"The traffic, first of all, but also the light. Now it's

changing. Come on." Olmedo led Sky across the wide avenue, tapping along with his cane.

"All right," said Sky when they reached the curb. "How did you do that?"

"You're not listening. Hear the buzz?"

It was hard to hear anything over the rush of cars, but yes, there was a faint something. A buzz, maybe.

"The green light is a little louder than the red light. And then you've got the switch box, over on the pole. You'll hear it click when it's going to change."

"Really?"

"Don't say 'really.' *Listen.* There's going to be a test."

Sky tried to block out the other sounds and hear the light. Was one faint buzz fainter than the other?

"Are you ready?"

"What do you mean?"

"Here's your test. Close your eyes."

Sky did as he was told. The swoosh of traffic seemed somehow louder, more dangerous.

"Now take my arm and lead me back across the street like a good Boy Scout."

Sky's eyes sprang open. "With my eyes *closed?*"

"What do you think?"

"We'll get killed!"

"I've crossed this street a thousand times, and I only got hit once. You probably remember that time."

"I can't do it!"

"Okay. Then good-bye. Toot sweet. It's been nice."

"No, listen. You just said you've done this a thousand times. I haven't done it even once!"

"Don't you think there was a first time for me, too?"

"But you can hear!"

"Oh, that's right, I forgot you're handicapped."

Sky was silent.

"So," said Olmedo. "Are we ready? I'm getting cold out here."

"You really think I can?"

"Sonny, I'm betting my life on it."

"All right, I'll try."

"Wait! Whatever you do, don't *try*."

"I see what you mean."

"Now listen and tell me what you hear."

"I hear a buzz. Sort of."

"Good boy."

The buzz went on for a while. Then there was another sound, closer.

"Is that the click?"

"That's the click."

The buzz resumed. Or another buzz.

"Is it green?"

"Go! It's not going to stay green forever."

Sky tripped off the curb and just managed to catch himself.

"Easy," said Olmedo.

"How do I know what direction?"

"I'll guide you. Just go!"

Sky hustled forward, his arm linked with Olmedo's. How wide was this street, anyway?

"If you open your eyes," said Olmedo, tapping along with his cane, "I will know it."

He would too, thought Sky. *But I* have *to look.*

Maybe not, maybe not. How much farther can it be?

"So you should know," said Olmedo, with a hint of something like concern in his voice, "we're halfway across and the light is changing."

"What!"

"But if you open your eyes, I will kill you. Let's run!" The blind man pulled Sky into a loping canter, just as the sound of gunning motors reached them and the first of several car horns.

"Remember!" shouted Olmedo over the rising noise. "I will kill you!"

Sky stumbled and half fell, but Olmedo's arm steadied him.

"Almost there, amigo!"

A warm stink of exhaust surrounded them like the breath of lions. Somewhere car brakes squealed.

"Come on!" Olmedo shouted, yanking Sky forward.

Suddenly, Sky tripped over a stone of some kind and fell headlong. Instinctively, he covered his head with his arms, sure he would be run over. His eyes opened. He was lying on the sidewalk.

"Get up, you're embarrassing me," said Olmedo. He was standing above him, breathing hard.

Sky winced. He had scraped his elbow badly. Grimacing, he sucked air in through his teeth. "Okay," he said.

The two of them set off along the sidewalk toward Olmedo's building and stopped in front of the door. Olmedo looked very tired. "This is where I get off."

"Could I ask you something?"

"Quick. I gotta lie down."

"Was there some purpose to what we just did over there?"

"You tell me."

"Well, I suppose you wanted me to learn how to listen."

Olmedo shook his head. "Not just listen. To listen as if your life *depended* on it. Big difference."

Sky nodded.

"Because if you can listen that way, then maybe one day you can play that way."

Max was already setting up when Sky arrived at Judson around seven thirty.

"A guy named Federico let me in."

Sky nodded.

"Cool place you got here."

"My sanctuary," said Sky.

Max smirked. "Literally."

"Larry coming?"

"Can't make it." Max was fitting his sizzle cymbal on its stand. "We'll just have to groove without a bass."

Sky noticed lately how many "cool" expressions had been creeping into Max's vocabulary. Probably all those Ferlinghetti and Ginsberg poems.

He sat at the piano and fooled around with some blues changes in F. Max slid behind the drums and joined in, using his brushes on the snare while his foot controlled the steady *chunk-ah* of the high hat. It was a nice easy sound, with a swing to it.

A half hour later Federico came up the stairs, followed by Suze in a floppy brown hat and woolen scarf.

"Hey," said Max, looking up from the drums.

"Don't stop," said Suze.

Sky had gotten up to find her a chair. If the choir actually used this loft, they did their singing standing up. All he could find was a dusty hi-fi speaker. She perched on it and pulled off the hat, letting her black hair tumble out behind her. Sky saw there was something different about her, then realized she was wearing more makeup than usual. Still understated, but she wasn't hiding. She looked, in fact, like she was on a date.

Rico gave her a frankly appreciative look, as if he hadn't really seen her at first. It was a cinch he had no idea she was fifteen.

"You cats are wailin'," Rico said, giving Sky an approving nod.

"Usually, we have a bass," said Max. He changed from brushes to sticks as Sky moved to a Latin rhythm for "Poinciana."

Federico ran his finger around the neckline of his black turtleneck. "I got my axe downstairs."

"You play?" said Max.

"Time to time."

"Well, go get it!"

In five minutes Rico returned wielding an enormous bass violin in a canvas case. He tuned up quickly, and then, at a sign from Sky, jumped into an up-tempo

"Lady Is a Tramp." It was obvious that he didn't play from "time to time." He was so fast and full of ideas that Sky and Max had to push themselves to match him. Larry Gar could be counted on to provide a dependable beat; but this guy—it was another world.

"Wow," said Suze, shaking her head, when they finished.

"Crazy, man," said Max.

"Hey," said Rico, "you staying for the party? Down in the community room. You should come." He looked from one to the other. "They even got a piano."

Sky looked at Suze, who laughed back at him. That was a yes.

They headed down a little early to set up. The room had its own entrance, a few steps below street level, and felt more clubby than churchy, with easy chairs and ashtrays and a nonchalant décor. Sky and Suze helped Max lug his drums while Federico toted the bass. Sometime before ten, people started showing up, many of them in blue jeans and bomber jackets. There were a lot of turtlenecks, such as Rico wore, but also a few guys in white shirts and skinny ties, and one cool character skulking about in dark glasses, as if the room weren't dark enough. Everyone looked to be five to twenty-five years older than Sky, but nobody cared. They wanted him to keep playing. No danger of anyone asking for "Tammy." Jazz was their meat, although they didn't seem to mind talking through it. Smoke hung in the air, not all of it tobacco. A girl who must have been twenty, maybe older, Sky thought, slid onto the piano bench and started talking to him while he and Rico traded eight-bar solos on "In Walked Bud." Pixie-haired and tipsy in her snug dress, she didn't notice that Sky wasn't answering her. When she left, called away by a guy with hair much longer than her own, her plastic glass of Chianti remained by the keyboard. Sky casually sipped at it between tunes. It wasn't his first drink. He'd had wine at Max's bar mitzvah two years ago and a couple of times since. He knew what was what.

Tonight was no bar mitzvah. After a few swallows Sky suddenly felt he understood the meaning of the word "cool." He was a cool cat. He was in Greenwich Village, and he was wailing.

What would Truscott make of him talking like that? he wondered briefly. What would he make of him talking at all?

Sky looked up to see a guy in his twenties—tousle-haired, handsome in a truck-driverish way—leaning an elbow on the piano and talking to Suze. His body was tilted away from her, but his eyes were excited and his gestures were big as he spoke, drawing her toward his leaning-away body as if saying, *I'm harmless, but don't you love me?*

Suze's expression was somewhere between amused and amazed. He would ask her a question and then answer a totally different, unasked question before she could reply. Max and Rico were demanding Sky's musical attention, so he missed most of the conversation, but it was something about poetry and how it would save the universe, or at least West Fourth Street. Then, to Sky's amazement, the guy's voice rose, and he began spouting lines of verse, his gestures growing wilder. People turned to listen.

"'I called to the angels of my generation!'" he cried, no longer leaning but rising to his full height, which wasn't all that tall, "'on the rooftops, in the alleyways, beneath the garbage and the stones . . .'"

Rico gave a significant nod to Sky, who somehow understood to abandon the tune he was playing and just follow the poet's voice. Sky's hands clambered up the keyboard, chord by clustered chord, till the poet yelled, "'*I screamed the name!* and they came . . .'"

Max did a quick press roll and hit the sizzle cymbal just as Sky struck a high, almost painful A-flat ninth.

"'. . . and gnawed the child's bones.'"

Quiet dissonance in the left hand, like animals rooting in the dark.

"'*I screamed the name: Beauty . . .*'"

Another upward clambering of golden chords while Rico spiraled into an ecstatic arpeggio on the bass.

"'Beauty Beauty Beauty.'"

Each word a higher major chord. A ping on Federico's bass and a ding on the triangle and the poem was over.

As applause burst out around them Sky realized that the poet was still staring into Suze's eyes and that she couldn't break away.

Beauty, beauty, beauty.

The man is dangerous, thought Sky, watching him bend forward and kiss Suze's fingertips like some sort of manic prince. A moment later he was grinning, pumping Federico's hand, then Max's, and finally Sky's.

"Hey, my man!" he said. "Name's Gregory. You are the end!"

This was a compliment Sky had not heard before, and he nodded warily.

"The absolute end! Hey, Allen!" he called to an intense-looking bearded guy standing nearby. "How about these cats?"

The bearded one came over and turned large and soulful eyes upon Sky. The impression of intensity was even greater close up, the eyes magnified by thick, dark-rimmed glasses, the front part of his head balding, as if to emphasize the lobes of his brain. It would not have surprised Sky to learn that the man was brilliant.

In an unexpectedly soft voice the beard said simply, "Immense."

Something about that single word, spoken quietly, was strangely moving to Sky.

"Why don't you do one?" said Gregory.

Allen just wagged his beard, no.

"Oh!" Gregory looked around with mischievous eyes. "He's going to make us beg him. Oh, please, great master!" He knelt on the floor.

The beard looked down at him. "You are a profoundly silly man."

"I know. Oh, I know."

"And you." Allen bent over the piano. "You play like Blake's angel."

Sky found himself blushing, although he had no idea what the guy was talking about.

"I'm Allen," he went on. "To whom am I speaking?"

"Sky."

"Sky!" The man's eyes widened. "That is *perfect*."

Again, Sky felt the weight of the words as something strangely significant. His name, it seemed, was perfect. He smiled and ducked his head.

Several people congregated around Allen, bearing him away to meet friends at the other side of the room. Max signaled to Sky. "You know who that *was*?"

"He said his name was Allen."

"Allen *Ginsberg*. He's the guy who wrote that poem."

"About climbing down from the Christmas tree?"

"No, no, the other one. He's famous. There was even a trial. Obscenity or something."

"What about his friend? The one who's been hitting on Suze. Is he obscene too?"

Max shrugged. "He's Gregory Corso. I don't know his stuff."

Sky scanned the room, but he didn't see Susan anywhere. He knew it was stupid to worry about her. "Back in a minute!" he said. The crowd was so dense, it was almost impenetrable. Making his way through, he tried to put out of his mind the idea of wild, hairy, obscene men getting their hands on Suze.

He found her at last, leaning against the back of an easy chair, talking seriously with Corso. He looked pretty harmless now. Boyish, even.

She looked up and smiled. "I was just telling Gregory about you."

"Me?"

"Your problem finding a place to practice."

"Bummer, man," said Corso, shaking his curly head. "And this gig at school . . ."

"The music assembly," Suze explained.

"Ah," said Sky. "The music assembly that wasn't."

"Your chick had this hairy idea. What if Allen and I showed up?"

"At *school*?"

"Dig. We could do some poems, and you and your pals could wail in the background, like the mad geniuses you are."

Sky looked at Suze. Her eyes were diamonds of excitement.

"That way," said Corso, "it would be, like, litter-ah-toor, dig?"

Sky looked down and shook his head. It would be amazing. A coup. It would shut up the jocks forever. "My dad won't go for it," he said in a murmur.

"Dinosaur, huh?" said Corso.

"Prehistoric."

"Wait," said Suze. "All he'd know is that some well-known poets are giving a reading and asked you to do a little background music."

It would never work. It was wonderful. She was beautiful. It would never work.

"Do you think it would work?" said Sky.

"It's only life and death," said Suze.

Corso grinned. "Is this chick a groove?"

Sky had settled himself back at the piano and was swinging into "Take the A Train" when a gust of cold air told him someone was coming in the door. People had been coming and going all night, and now, just past midnight, the room was packed with bodies. The laughter was louder than before, the arguments more vehement. A few people were even trying to dance. Sky nodded to Rico to take a bass solo, which gave him a moment to knock back the last swallow of wine.

He happened to look up then, the plastic glass still at his lips. He almost choked. A round, strangely tanned, astonished-looking face was glancing sharply around the room, looking for someone. The man's eyes suddenly locked on Sky's.

Sky's fingers left the keyboard as if to deny that he'd ever been playing; but of course, that was foolish. He watched his father move toward him the way someone tied to the tracks would watch an oncoming locomotive. In those slow-motion seconds Sky found himself focusing on Quinn's bald dome, so different from Allen's. Why would one man's baldness make him look like an intellectual while another's made him look like a yellow-headed bulldog?

The bulldog knocked roughly against a girl's shoulder, making the wine lurch from her glass. He arrived at the piano.

"So!" said Quinn, glaring down. "Is this the church function you were talking about?"

Sky was split between anger and terror. "What are you doing here?"

"Never mind. You're coming home!"

Max stopped playing, and then Federico did too. The place quieted down.

"Dad, what's wrong?"

"We'll talk in the cab."

Sky stared straight ahead. This was unbelievable.

"Come on, I said!" Quinn barked. "Don't make a scene."

"Who's making a scene?" Sky mumbled.

"Hi, Mr. Schuyler!" came an overbright female voice. "I'm Susan."

"You're . . . ?"

"Sue Matheson. Sky's date. I'm so glad to—"

"Does your father know what's going on here?"

"I . . . Of course." Suze was not easily daunted, but she was caught off guard.

"I don't think he does. Not that it's my concern." He turned to his son. "Alec. Now!"

"Dad, for godsake!"

Quinn grabbed his son's arm, twisting it painfully as he dragged him to his feet.

"Ow!" Sky didn't fight. His humiliation was so profound, he had tears in his eyes. Allen, Gregory, Max, Rico, Suze were all witnessing this. They were seeing Sky being treated like a naughty boy and led off for a spanking.

It was cold outside, which only made Sky's tears hotter. A cab was growling by the curb.

"In!"

Sky didn't move, so Quinn shoved him, then went

around the other side. Soon they were speeding uptown.

Neither spoke for some time.

Finally: "*Why,* Dad?"

"Because there are still some parents like Bob Matheson who care about their children. He called up tonight wanting to know more about this 'church function.' I said I'd look into it. Surprise. No church function."

"It was a party held in the church," said Sky.

"It was a beatnik free-for-all! What did I tell you about jazz? You end up hanging around lowlifes. You *become* a lowlife!"

"It was perfectly—"

"I promised your mother I would take care of you, and by God, that's what I'm going to do! And don't tell me that was Pepsi you were drinking!"

Sky couldn't answer, not because he felt beaten down, but because he was afraid of what would come out if he spoke.

"Dad," he said, his voice low with fury. He was watching the lights of Fourteenth Street whiz past. "Listen to me. This one time in your life *listen* to me. I am a jazz musician. It is what I am."

"Like *hell*!"

The cab stopped for a light at Twenty-fifth, and Sky popped open the door. His father grabbed his arm as Sky struggled, half out of the car.

"Let go!"

But Quinn was stronger than Sky had realized, and the boy felt himself being dragged back. In desperation, he slammed his fist down on his father's forearm. Quinn roared in pain, his grip loosening, and Sky tore free.

"You go, you don't come *back*!" Quinn yelled.

"Fine!" Sky slammed the door.

Sky knew he couldn't walk the streets all night, unless he wanted to end up as a lump in an alley. He ducked down the staircase to the Twenty-third Street station, glad for its faint, sour-smelling warmth, and took the first train that came. Soon it was rocketing north, howling through its underground world. Sky hugged himself, his hands in his armpits. The racket outside and the turmoil in his head made it hard to think.

Was he really not going home? *Ever?*

The train skipped some stops and ground to a teeth-rattling halt at others as it continued through upper Manhattan and into the Bronx. A few tired-looking people got on and others stumbled off, until Sky was the only passenger left. Dark columns flashed by, illuminated by showers of sparks as the train took a screeching curve. At last it coasted to a stop, sighed a great humid sigh, and flung open its doors.

Sky had no intention of wandering through the wilds of outlying boroughs. He wedged himself in a corner seat and closed his eyes. After awhile the train heaved another sigh, threw the doors closed, and . . . nothing. Then the lights went off.

What if it's here for the night? Sky thought, looking around at the station sign: VAN CORTLAND PARK, 242ND STREET. He dug into his pocket and counted his money in the dim light that came from the platform. Seven dollars and change, not enough to do anything. His father's face loomed before him, swollen with anger. Could he go back to that?

Just then the lights came on and the train slid from the station, picking up speed as it retraced its route south. Somewhere around Cathedral Parkway, Sky dozed off, waking at Canal Street in lower Manhattan. A painful stiffness gripped his neck, and he rubbed at it with his fingers.

Finally, the train reached South Ferry, as far south as you can get without actually falling into the harbor. There the engine cut off, and the lights went out again. It made Sky think of the moment of silence that people are always calling for to honor a dead person. Except Sky was the dead person. His old life was over, and he was alone in a dark metal container, waiting for hell to start in earnest.

In a few minutes the engine revved up again, and his eyes drifted closed. Sky lost track of the number of times he went back and forth, but around five in the morning he realized he needed to pee. He was also famished. At Times Square he jumped out and climbed the long stairs to the street.

It was still dark as he set out down Forty-second, past closed storefronts and pornographic movie houses. One of the saddest sights was an abandoned car dealership near Eighth Avenue. Some optimist had announced in block letters across the show window:

FIRST SPUTNIK
THEN FLYING SAUCERS
NOW EDSEL!

Progress, thought Sky, peering through the dusty pane. *See where it gets you?* Everybody was always telling him how great the future would be. From what he could see, the future was an Edsel, the biggest bomb the Ford Motor Company had ever produced.

He shivered and hurried on. By Port Authority he found an open coffee shop, garish with neon. In the men's room he examined his face in the mirror and slicked back his hair with wet hands. He remembered it was Friday. His books were at home. Also the Shakespeare paper, all typed up and ready to hand in.

Sky straddled a stool at the counter. Seven and change, he remembered, and kept himself to a cup of coffee and an English muffin, lots of jelly on the side. He watched the counterman lay three strips of bacon on a big plate of eggs and hash browns and set it in front of a policeman, the only other customer in the place. It smelled almost painfully good.

Sky nibbled his muffin, making it last. He noticed the officer glance at his watch and stand up, calling out thanks and heading to the door. Two bacon strips lay untouched on the plate. The waiter went in the back, leaving Sky alone. Slowly, Sky stood up, edging along the counter till he was beside the plate. He checked the door to see if anyone was coming in. He rested his hand on the countertop.

"Want anything else?"

Sky jumped. "Uh . . . I guess not."

The waiter cleared away the plate with the bacon and wrote up a check. Coffee and muffin, ninety-five cents. Sky could leave a tip and still have six dollars left.

That English paper was bothering him. He didn't know why, but it bothered him more at this moment than the question of where he was going to sleep tonight. He could see it sitting there on the coffee table in the living room, beside his briefcase.

Holding closed the neck of his windbreaker, Sky headed east along Forty-second. He had never been out walking at dawn before. Something about that vague first light gave a look of innocence to the disgraceful old buildings. Continuing east, he was struck suddenly by direct sunlight and had to glance aside. Trucks grumbled past. A taxi honked furiously at a fuming bus. The moment of grace was over.

It was a long walk home, but Sky still arrived too early. He'd have to wait till his father left for work, around 8:15, another forty-five minutes. What was the old pug doing? Cracking his knuckles? Folding the newspaper into quarters and reading it one fold at a time? By now he'd be biting into his cinnamon toast, his ears doing that thing they did. Sky scuffed along the sidewalk, watching the workers on Third Avenue starting up their machines, getting back to the job of tearing down the El. He walked around the block. Then he walked around the block again. Finally, he stood across the street outside the Pinehurst Garage and waited.

At 8:20 the white front door opened and Quinn Schuyler appeared, buttoning his trench coat. Although Sky had expected him, it was sort of a shock. He hadn't thought of his father as that short or, frankly, that old. Sky watched him head off toward Lexington. He moved slowly, something vague about him. This was not the brisk, decisive man who had dominated Sky's childhood.

Did I do this to him? Sky thought with a pang.

He did it to his own damn self.

Sky crossed the street, let himself in, and pounded

up the stairs to the third-floor entrance to the apartment. Why did he feel like a thief?

He gathered up the English paper and briefcase
from the coffee table and ran to his room on the top
floor to grab a toothbrush, a change of underwear, and
another shirt. In the bureau he found his money box
and emptied it. Eight dollars and pennies.

This is my own money, he reminded himself. *I am not
stealing anything.*

Five minutes later he was on the street again, his
briefcase bulging as he headed to Third to catch the
uptown bus. It was slow arriving.

"Hey," he heard behind him.

Dave Rubin was waving from the door of the deli.

"Hi, Mr. Rubin." Suddenly, he remembered how
hungry he was. His view was partly blocked by the El's
dark columns, but no bus seemed to be coming. He
ducked inside. "You got an apple turnover?"

"Sure I got. Why, you missed breakfast? I'll make
you something."

"I can't wait. I'm late for school."

"Better you miss school than you miss breakfast. I'll
be quick."

Sky saw the bus roar by outside.

Rubin noticed his look. "So now you're not in so
much of a hurry."

"I guess not." Sky watched the old man crack two eggs

on the griddle. In three minutes he'd wrapped up a fried egg sandwich on rye and slipped a pickle on the side.

Who eats a pickle for breakfast? thought Sky, opening his wallet.

"Never mind," Dave said.

"What do you mean? I've got to pay you."

He shook his wobbly jowls. "I don't know how much longer I'll be seeing you. We got our notice."

"What!"

"This whole block's coming down."

Sky stared.

"Renewal, they call it. We been here forty-two years and we're being renewed."

"Can they do that?"

Mr. Rubin shrugged. He looked out the front window at a growling bulldozer. "That machine I don't like," he said.

"I hate it," said Sky.

Mr. Rubin gave him a long look, then broke it with a smile. "Go, you'll be late."

"It isn't fair."

"Fair, shmair. Here, don't forget your coffee."

Sky had missed first period, which was Latin. Not too serious. At his locker he ran into Max.

"You all right, man?" Max was looking at him gravely.

"I look that bad?"

"You look like hell."

"Long story," Sky murmured, hoping to cut it short. But his body betrayed him, and to his mortification he found his eyes filling with tears. "I'm okay," he said. "It's stupid."

Max steered him out the door to the flagstone courtyard. They waited for a fourth grader to run past into the Lower School. "Talk," Max said when they were alone.

Sky blew out a sigh and told him some of what had happened. Before he finished, Max said, "You'll stay at my place tonight."

"That's the first place he'll look."

Max nodded. "You're right."

"Assuming he is looking."

"Don't worry, he's looking. He called during first period. Miss Dowell saw me in the hall and sent me over to see if you were in Latin. Here, let me give you some money."

"I'm all right."

"Don't be stupid." Max pulled out his wallet. "It's only four dollars, but . . ."

"Really, I'm okay." Sky flinched as the bell went off.

"We'll talk at lunch," said Max. The friends hurried inside to their different classes. They didn't see each other again till fourth period: Truscott.

"Well, ladies and gentlemen, let's hand in our papers." Mark Truscott stood at the front of the class, arms folded, watching the students pass their papers to the front. Sky felt a grim satisfaction. Truscott would find some reason not to like his essay, but Sky had done his best, and against odds that his teacher would never understand, he had handed it in.

"I look forward to a weekend of pleasurable reading," said Truscott, rising on his toes and lowering himself again. He held the pile of papers as if weighing it, then picked one out. "Why not give myself a preview?"

He read the paper aloud. It was about *Romeo and Juliet*, by a boy suggesting commonsense ways the lovers could have avoided their fate. Truscott didn't waste his sarcasm here but went on to others more worthy of it. Finally he extracted a substantial paper, holding it by its stapled corner as one might hold up a laboratory mouse by its tail. "This one, let's see, is by—well, never mind who it's by. Nice long title: 'Rejecting the One You Love: The Sad Case of Hamlet and Ophelia.' Now, there's a subject!"

As he began reading, the students glanced around trying to figure out who the unlucky author was. It was obvious Truscott was prowling for prey. There was that dangerous smile of his, already on the edge of mockery.

And yet, as he read along, the smile began to fade. "'Does Hamlet's nasty treatment of Ophelia,'" he read in the second paragraph, "'come from suspicion, or from a disgust for all women, or from what Coleridge calls "a wild upworking of love"? I'm guessing it's a little of all three, but mostly I'm with Coleridge on this one.'"

"Coleridge?" Truscott interrupted himself, his eyes scissoring the room. "What tenth grader would know Coleridge's Shakespeare criticism?" He leafed to the back of the paper and grunted. Everyone waited. Truscott prided himself on his skill at catching plagiarists. This would mean serious trouble. A failing grade would be the least of it.

He looked down, contemplating his gleaming shoes, then up at the ceiling. "Let's go on a bit," he said. "'They say that love is a clear and innocent emotion. But that is true only for clear and innocent minds like Ophelia's.'" Truscott's frown deepened. "'For darker minds like Hamlet's, or like people we've all known in our lives, it can be hard to admit such feelings. What if the person we love laughs at us? Rejects us? People faced with that possibility could resort to "a willful self-tormenting irony," as Coleridge puts it. They may even reject the person they love.'"

Truscott colored. "Coleridge again!" He flipped to the footnotes. "Again, correctly footnoted." He adjusted his tortoise-shell glasses and read on to the end. "Well, what do we think?" he said, giving the cover page a flick with his finger. "Anyone venture an opinion?"

No one ventured an opinion. Who, in Truscott's class, would venture an opinion?

Sky raised his hand.

Everyone in the class turned. Steve Glass whispered something to Gertrude Somerville, but she wasn't listening.

"Yes, Mr. Schuyler?" said Truscott.

"I think it's goddam brilliant."

A collective gasp sucked the air out of the room. The mute boy had spoken. And he had used a curse word.

Truscott seemed to falter. "I agree with you, Mr. Schuyler," he said, clearing his throat. "Informally written, slangy in spots, but—as you say—damn brilliant indeed. And now, class, since it's unlikely we'll be able to top this paper, I'm going to let you go a little early."

At first no one moved.

"Go on, go on, everybody," said Truscott. "Shoo! Miss Matheson, may I see you after class?"

The students filed out as if in a dream.

As Sky entered the cafeteria Max signaled him from their usual table in the back. "What got into you today?" Max said.

"Nothing."

"What do you mean, 'nothing'?"

Sky shrugged.

"You should sleep in the subways more often."

Sky paused. "Truscott doesn't matter," he said.

"Of course he doesn't matter. He's just got everybody thinking he does."

"I mean, what's he going to do?"

"Exactly."

The two were silent. "I assume Suze wrote the paper," said Sky.

"Ask her." Max was watching Suze make her way through the jostling crowd. In her white sweater she looked delightfully out of place, like a lily in the middle of a bean field. "Hey," he said.

"Hey." She set down her tray and took her usual seat between them. She turned to Sky. "Did you *really* stay out all night last night? Max told me—"

Sky nodded.

"That's *incredible*! You going home tonight?" She saw him hesitate. "You have to! I mean . . . *don't* you?"

He didn't answer. He didn't know what to say.

"I don't blame you for not wanting to. Sometimes my family gives me the willies."

Sky remembered Mr. Matheson's voice on the phone talking to Quinn. "I can believe you."

"Her father," said Max quietly, "is just slightly overprotective."

"We know it's worse than that," said Suze.

"Also," Max said, "he doesn't care for Jews."

"That's true, I'm afraid. But I'm not going to be living there forever. Same with you, Sky. In a few years—"

"A few years!"

"A few years is not that long. Then you'll be out on your own."

"In the cab last night," said Sky slowly, "I told my dad. I said to him, 'I am a jazz musician. That's who I am.'"

"Yeah?" said Max. "And?"

"He said, 'Like hell you are!'"

His friends were silent.

"That's when I got out."

"Still . . . ," Suze began.

"Hey, guys!" It was Jill Coverton, clasping a pile of books to her chest. She was also balancing a slice of peach pie and an open carton of milk. "Can I join you?"

"Sure," said Max, moving over.

But Jill sat next to Sky, slopping her books on the table. "You were amazing in class today. What came over you?"

"I don't know," Sky murmured. It was true.

"You just shot your hand right up there!"

Sky smiled and looked down. There was no way to tell her that what he'd done was not an act of defiance, but an act of indifference.

Jill cut into the peach pie with her fork. "So you guys want to go for a soda or something afterward?"

"After what?" said Max.

"The dance! It's a week from today, for godsake!" She laughed.

"Oh." Max looked at the others. "What do you think?"

"Perfect," said Suze.

"This is going to be *so fun*!"

Sky looked at Jill. She was an unusual kind of pretty. Athletic though she was, her heavy-lidded eyes made her look like she'd just woken from a dream. She'd be cozy to curl up with.

They talked awhile about the dance and whether they should connect up beforehand. Then Jill glanced at her small white-gold Bulova. "Whoops, gotta go."

She stood and tilted her head back for a last glug of milk. She took too much, and it overflowed down the curve of her smile onto her sweater.

Sky jumped to his feet, grabbing a couple of paper napkins. He hesitated a second, his hand hovering. "Here!" he blurted.

She took the napkins and dabbed at her chest while Sky reached for more napkins to wipe off the French book. Her other books hadn't escaped either.

"Cheese!" said Jill. "Klutz that I am!"

Sky dried the edge of the last book, a dog-eared

paperback with a yellow cover, and handed it to her, noticing the title, *Selected Writings of Samuel Taylor Coleridge.*

He gave her a stunned look. She blushed.

"Thanks," she said, her voice lowering. "For *everything.*" Then she turned away.

"A bundle of energy, that girl," said Max.

"Quite a dancer, too," said Suze. "I don't think you'll be able to keep up with her, Max."

Sky watched Jill's dark blond ponytail bobbing through the crowd till she reached the door and disappeared.

As the end of the school day approached, Sky was feeling more and more edgy. Other kids were passing notes and shoving, as if it were just a normal Friday, which it was far from.

"Seven minutes to go," groaned Peter Wendt, glancing at the clock. "Get me out of here!"

Seven minutes to go, Sky repeated to himself, his heart dropping. He had two immediate problems: what to do with the rest of his life and what to do about Suze Matheson. Truscott had asked her to stay after school today and go over ideas for the *Review*. She couldn't think of a reason to say no.

"I'll go with you," Sky had told her; but she just shook her head. She was right. It would look ridiculous showing up with a chaperone.

Privately, Sky made his plans. He lingered in the tenth-grade homeroom until the last student thudded down the stairs, then slipped into the coat closet and pulled the sliding door most of the way shut. He sat in the dark among forgotten galoshes with his briefcase beside him, waiting. It was uncomfortably warm. The closet, a varnished plywood afterthought, had been set around one of the building's heat vents, and hot air was puffing in. Sky felt his long night catching up with him. He fought back a yawn.

At last he heard steps and then a male voice, followed by Suze's laugh. It was her dutiful laugh, Sky realized, far from the delighted yelp she let out when she was with friends. Truscott spoke again. A chair leg groaned as it was pulled across the floor.

"I like your ideas, far as I can make them out," he was saying. "We just can't afford them."

Suze said something indistinct.

"This isn't the yearbook, remember," he replied. "That's a whole different budget. They can *afford* photos."

"I was just thinking of little, postage-stamp-size ones," said Suze, her voice stronger now. "You know, at the head of each story."

"It would be nice. We can't afford it."

"It would mean a lot to the kids."

"I'm sure it would."

"And the glossy cover?"

"Same problem."

"Oh, but—" Her voice audibly drooped.

"Wait, wait," he said, catching himself. "Before I keep saying no, why don't you tell me your ideas, and then we'll see what we can do and what we can't."

"So then you can say one great big no at the end?"

Truscott chuckled. Sky had never heard this man chuckle before. Snicker, yes.

"Let me think about this," Truscott said. "There may be something I can do. You know the expression 'Borrow from Peter to pay Paul'?"

"As long as Peter doesn't mind."

"Maybe Peter doesn't have to know."

"Can you do that?"

"I can't promise anything."

"Oh, I know!"

Encouraged, Suze began explaining her ideas. Sky couldn't hear much of what she said, but she obviously had in mind quite a different publication from the dowdy, staple-bound rag he was used to seeing around school.

Typical Suze, he thought, slumping against the back of the closet. The voices were quieter now, the words hard to distinguish, just an occasional expulsive laugh from Truscott and a bright "Of course!" from Suze. Sky let his eyes close.

The thump of a desk drawer brought him suddenly awake. How long had he been out?

"Your father said *that*?" Truscott's voice cut through the air. "Doesn't he trust you?"

Sky didn't catch her response.

"But he's letting you go to the dance, isn't he?"

"As long as I don't go with anyone . . . undesirable."

He gave a short laugh. "Who, at Harmon Prep of all places, would be 'undesirable'?"

Sky stood up slowly, careful not to make noise. Through the narrow opening, he could see Suze at the teacher's desk, an elbow on a pile of manuscripts, her chin resting on her fist. Beside her Truscott lounged in his shirtsleeves, his tie loosened, his arm lying along the back of her chair.

"Oh," she said, "my dad could give you quite a list."

"And you really think he wouldn't want you to be editor of the *Review*?"

"He doesn't like me drawing attention to myself."

"My dear, you can hardly help that!"

"Well," she said, coloring, "it was just easier to tell him I'm 'on the staff.'"

"He should be proud of you!"

"My father means well," she said. "He's just trying to protect me from the big bad world."

Truscott took off his glasses and flipped them onto a stack of old *Harmon Review*s. "Any part particularly?" he said. "Of the big bad world?"

"Men, mostly."

"Yes, well, you can hardly blame him for that!"

She blushed.

"I mean, you're a very lovely girl." He gave her shoulder a squeeze through the fuzzy white sweater.

"You can't be unaware of the effect you have."

He gave another squeeze for emphasis, then let his hand lie there. Suze glanced at it. "Your father's right," Truscott went on. "You shouldn't be too trusting. There are wolves around the sheepfold. Who are you going to the dance with, if I may ask?"

She looked at him in surprise. "I'm going with Sky."

"Mr. Schuyler! Good choice! Well, a safe choice. Definitely not a wolf. More a puppy, wouldn't you say?"

Sky, peeping from the closet, felt the breath go out of him. He waited for her answer.

"I—I don't know," she stammered.

"Just the sort of fellow your father would approve of."

"That's not fair!"

"Harmless? Tongue-tied?"

"Mr. Truscott, what do you have against Sky?"

"Me? Nothing in the world! I just like my steak with more juice in it."

"You don't know him."

"How can I? He won't speak to me."

"He spoke today."

He paused. "You're right. He spoke today. Today he was sensational."

"He's got plenty of juice in him, Mr. Truscott."

"I'm glad to hear it. And for heaven's sake, call me Mark! I hope you and I have gotten past these idiotic formalities."

"All right," she said in a low voice.

Steak with more juice in it, thought Sky. He bunched his fists.

Truscott was silent.

Suze concentrated on the desktop, examining its surface for imperfections.

"I suppose you have lots of admirers," he said finally. Almost idly, he began stroking her shoulder.

She shrugged. Sky had the impression she was trying to shrug his hand away.

Truscott gazed at her face in profile. If looks were touches, he'd have been all over her. "I wonder," he said at last, "how many of those admirers have any idea whom they're admiring."

She frowned at the desk.

"Your friend Mr. Schuyler, for instance. No doubt he fantasizes about you endlessly. But does he know who you are?"

"Do *you*?" she said, turning to Truscott and giving him a straight look. "Do you know who I am?"

"I think I do."

She opened her mouth but didn't speak. From where Sky was, she looked afraid.

"Shall I tell you?" Truscott continued gently rubbing her shoulder.

She looked down at the desk again.

"Oh, let me." His smile was fatherly. "First, the

obvious: You are a person of intelligence. Some other girls avoid you or talk behind your back because, through no fault of your own, you happen to be more beautiful than they are and a good deal brighter. Some of the boys won't approach you because, frankly, you scare the hell out of them. Am I getting warm?"

Suze took a deep breath. "Go on."

"But the main truth about you . . ." He paused, searching her face for confirmation. "The main truth is that you have a passion. Your father doesn't understand this passion. Your friends, I'm betting, don't know anything about it. But I do, my dear."

She raised her eyes and looked at him silently as he pushed a strand of hair back from her face.

"I have seen your poems. I've read your stories. And I've seen the hunger in them."

"Oh," she murmured.

"Yes, and the talent." He let the back of his fingers brush against her cheek in a light caress. "I believe you can be a writer. A fine one."

She closed her eyes, as if to let the words sink deeply in. "Do you?"

"Isn't that what you want?" His hand slid past her ear and grazed her neck. "To be a writer?"

She didn't reply. Sky thought she looked hypnotized.

"It is, isn't it?"

"Oh God," she whispered.

"You want it, don't you?" His voice was soft and deep and kind.

"So much."

Sky, across the room, was in turmoil. Should he announce himself? Should he break this horrible spell?

"I can help you," the teacher's voice continued.

"Can you?" Suze was staring at the monogram on his shirt pocket.

"If you want me to." His fingers again grazed her cheek. "Do you?" His thumb lightly traced the curve of her lips, and her mouth opened slightly. "Do you want me to help you?"

"Yes."

"Do you?"

"Yes."

He pulled her toward him as he tilted his head, meeting her mouth with his.

Sky was stunned. *Hit him! Slap him!*

The kiss went on for a while. It might have gone on longer, but Truscott made the mistake of pushing his luck. His hand, which had been caressing her shoulder and neck, began to explore further.

She pushed him away. "Mark," she said. "No."

"Susan, Susan, Susan." He moved in for another kiss.

"No, Mark, I can't."

"Your father wouldn't approve?"

"*I* wouldn't approve."

He gave her a long look. "Very well." He released her and leaned away. "I misjudged."

Her hands trembling, she began gathering her many papers.

"I thought we had a special bond," he said. "I thought you wanted my help."

She looked at him with alarm. "I do. We do . . ."

"No, Susan. I was expecting too much."

"No, no, I didn't mean . . ."

"What, dear?"

"I didn't mean we couldn't *work* together."

"Without trust?"

She didn't know what to say.

"I thought we could go beyond the conventions. Cut through those foolish barriers between teacher and student." He shook his head.

"Are you saying you won't help me?"

"I'm saying I'm disappointed. Now you'd better go. It's getting late."

"But . . ."

"What is it?"

She sighed. "You're right. I'd better go."

Good girl! thought Sky from his hiding place. *Get out of there!*

Suze stood and began stuffing manuscripts into her briefcase while Truscott looked up at her from his chair. She was reaching over for her geometry book when he caught her around the waist and buried his face in her stomach.

She gasped. Her hands, one holding the briefcase, the other the book, instinctively flew out to the side.

"Mark, no!"

But he pulled her tighter against him. She struggled to free herself.

"Quit it!"

He slid his hand under the back of her sweater.

Three things happened at nearly the same moment:

Truscott glanced up in amazement to see Alec Schuyler bearing down on him.

Suze, partly recovered from her shock, brought the manuscript-stuffed briefcase down on Truscott's neck.

And suddenly, all three of them heard a strange clanking sound coming from the stairwell.

They froze where they were. The clanking grew louder, and then the cleaning lady, known to all as Nessie, hove into sight lugging a mop and a sloshing bucket of water.

Truscott jumped to his feet, snatching his tweed jacket from the back of the chair. He was smoothing back his hair when she stuck her head in the door.

"Oh!" she said in her high voice. "I thought I was alone!"

"Just finishing up, Nessie. We'll be out of your way in a minute."

Sky wasn't waiting a minute. He strode over and grabbed his coat and briefcase from the closet, then took Suze's arm and steered her quickly from the room.

"Um, good night, Nessie," said Suze as they started down the stairs.

In the entrance hall the two friends pulled open the heavy door, then the black metal gate, and stepped outside into the first snowstorm of the season.

13

They were halfway up the street, the snow skittering around them, when Sky saw that Suze was crying. He stopped and folded her against him. He felt her tremble.

"It's all right," he said.

"I'm such a baby."

"Come on." He led her to the drugstore on the corner of Ninety-sixth Street. "How about a hot chocolate?" he said. "My treat."

"I'd like that."

They slid into a booth and for a while just stared out the window, watching the snow increase and the light diminish. Even after their order came, Sky didn't say much, and Suze didn't expect him to. That was fine, but there was so much she didn't know. "You mean you were there the *whole time?*" she said finally.

"Call me suspicious."

"I call you my knight in shining armor."

They lapsed into silence.

"So," said Sky, still amazed by it all. "Looks like we were right about Truscott."

"I guess."

"You guess?"

"Maybe he just got carried away."

Sky wasn't sure he understood her.

"I knew I shouldn't have worn that sweater," she murmured into her cup.

"Suze, listen to me. You could have worn a potato sack . . ."

"No, it was just too, you know, formfitting."

Sky didn't know how to answer. She had never worn a formfitting sweater in her life. "Suze, listen. Truscott is your teacher."

She raised her eyes reluctantly. "I guess what I'm most disappointed about is my brilliant career. I thought he was going to help me."

"He was helping himself. He was even coming back for seconds."

She looked at him bleakly. "He was, wasn't he? Oh God. Well, I guess that does it for me editing the *Review*."

"Maybe you don't have to give it up."

Suze gave him a look that said, *I don't really have to respond to that, do I?* She drained the dregs of her cocoa and set her cup down. "What about you?" she said. "What are you going to do?"

He shrugged.

"You *can't* wander the streets all night in the snow. It's too Hans Christian Andersen."

"Corny, you think?" He smiled.

"Way too corny. Anyway, if you freeze to death, who'll take me to the dance?"

"I don't think you'll have trouble finding volunteers. Max, for one."

"He's taking Jill."

"On the rebound."

"You think so?" The thought seemed to give her pleasure. "He's my other protector. I've got such good protectors."

"We try."

"But who will protect *you*?"

"I'm all right."

"Be serious, Sky. You've *got* to go home."

"I may."

She was about to insist again, but she saw his look and held off.

The streetlights were just coming on as they stepped outside. Sky waited with Suze till a bus came along, but he hung back as she stepped on.

"Not coming?" She looked alarmed.

"In awhile."

"Call me. I want to know where you are."

"If I can."

The accordion-shaped doors started folding closed.

"Don't forget!"

He watched the bus head down Columbus in a

cloud of exhaust. Why hadn't he grabbed a warmer coat this morning when he was home? And gloves, for godsake. Shivering, he hustled to Broadway and caught the downtown subway. At least he could get in an hour of practicing at Judson before he had to decide anything.

Sky watched the underground girders fly past the window and tried not to think of the kiss. He'd never seen anyone kiss a girl that way except in the movies. And she'd let him—that was the odd thing—for seconds and seconds. Did she think she was the first one to be so honored?

By the time Sky got off and climbed up to street level, the snow had begun sticking. Overfilled trash cans were looking like snow cones. No Parking signs were nearly illegible. He scuffled down Fourth Street, head down, briefcase in one hand, the other hand jammed in his pocket, till he came to Judson Church.

It was locked.

He trotted around to the side entrance but found that locked as well. It hurt to rap on the door with his cold knuckles, but then he heard a latch turn. The door swung inward, revealing Federico in a hooded sweat suit.

"Amigo!"

"Hi, Rico."

"You look cold."

Sky stepped inside gratefully. "Thought I'd practice a little."

"Practice all you want. Everything's been cancelled for tonight."

Sky headed to the choir loft. He didn't click on the lamp immediately, but stood in the semidarkness looking out over the sanctuary. Through the windows the vague light of late-afternoon snow mingled with the glow of a streetlamp. There was something about standing in an empty church, with all that silence below him, that made him feel hopeful, like maybe a way could be found.

"You okay?"

Sky looked around to see Federico outlined against the light from the stairway.

"Yeah, man. Just about to get started."

Rico came over. "Sometimes I come up here by myself and just sit."

"Yeah."

"Sure you're okay?"

"Well," said Sky, snapping on the little goosenecked lamp on the piano, "actually, I was wondering if you know a place I could stay tonight."

"Stay here. There's a real comfortable sofa downstairs."

"Really?"

"Sometimes I stay myself."

"Maybe I will. Thanks." Sky slid onto the piano bench and started running through scales. His hands felt as clumsy as stones. "Guess I'm still cold."

"You want some tea? I was making some."

"That would be great."

Rico left Sky to his scales. After awhile the notes came easier, even with the strange fingering Olmedo wanted him to use.

Before long Rico reappeared with two steaming mugs, just as Sky started working on his new piece, "Circle of Rain." He'd had a scattering of ideas over the past few days and jotted them down in the composition book he carried in his windbreaker.

"I don't know that one."

"It doesn't exist yet."

Rico looked over Sky's shoulder at the comp book. "Oh, I love it!"

"The bridge is weak."

"You think so?"

"We've heard these changes a million times."

"F-sharp minor to F-minor seventh?" Rico shook his head. "I don't think so."

"I'm not good at this."

"You're not only good, you're over here in a damn snowstorm *practicing*." He turned and gave a little wave over his shoulder as he headed downstairs.

Sky put in another hour before the loneliness of his

situation caught up with him. He went down to see if Federico knew a cheap place to eat in the neighborhood.

"Ever try the Lion's Head? Great chili. Maybe I'll go with you."

Sky's ears were stinging by the time they reached the *Village Voice* building on Sheridan Square. The Lion's Head was two doors down. "Here we are," said Federico, leading the way in.

The place was crowded and smoky and the talk loud. "Hey, Rico," called out the bartender.

"Hey, Irish."

"Can't serve your friend, you know."

Rico looked at Sky as if just noticing how young he looked. "Well, can we at least get some of your famous chili into him? He's a starving musician."

"Starving musicians always welcome." The big man named Irish leaned over and shook Sky's hand.

"Starving poets too," said a skinny fellow surrounding a beer at the bar.

"Hey, Joel," said Rico. "Meet Sky."

The man glanced up from his stool. Not a handsome guy—a bit of the mongrel about him—but his lively eyes made you like him right away. He shook Sky's hand. "Picking the fruit a little green, aren't you, Rico?"

Rico laughed comfortably. "No, no." He glanced at Sky.

"Attaboy," said Joel.

Sky wasn't sure what they were talking about.

"Joel claims he's a poet," said Rico, "but he really writes for that rag upstairs."

"You write for the *Voice?*" said Sky, impressed. He read the paper all the time. It was the only one that told you what jazz was where.

"Yeah, I had to escape just now. Editor's on the warpath."

"Did he want you to use actual grammar this time?"

"No, he's cool about that."

"Joel doesn't use capital letters," Rico explained. "He hasn't gotten that far in his education."

"Let's say I'm not a capitalist," said Joel.

"Hate to interrupt," said Irish, leaning his elbows on the bar, "but I think you boys better go sit in the back. I'd like to keep my license."

Rico gave a thumbs-up to Joel and steered Sky past the jukebox to a small table in the back. Stan Getz's saxophone cut through the smoke with "I Should Care."

"So where do you live?" said Rico after the chili was set steaming before them, roofed with grated cheddar.

"Upper East Side."

"Mn." Rico was biting into a piece of crusty Italian bread. "What's the scene up there?"

Sky smiled wanly. "I wouldn't exactly call it a scene."

"Well, what do you do up there?"

"I come down here."

"Mn." He bit off another piece. "Is this stuff good or what?"

"It's great."

"They got food like this on your Upper Snotty East Side?"

"There's one place I like. It's a deli."

"A good deli is worth something."

"It's going out of business."

"So why don't you move down here? I think you belong."

"I'd like to." For a moment the idea was so deeply tempting that Sky's voice faltered. "I'm not sure what my dad would say about it."

"I left home when I was sixteen. Never looked back."

"Really?"

"My parents couldn't handle who I was."

Sky watched the man eat. Finally, Rico looked up. "How about you?"

"My dad," Sky began, then paused, changing what he was about to say. "My dad means well. I really think he means well."

"The road to hell is paved with good intentions."

"No kidding."

"Anyway," said Rico, wiping his mouth, "I was

lucky. Things worked out. I met a man who took me in and treated me well. We stayed together five years, which is like an eternity in the homosexual world."

Sky had been swallowing his Coke and choked on it.

Rico looked at him in surprise. "You didn't figure that out?"

Sky was still coughing.

"Man! I thought I was so obvious. Don't tell me you never met a fag before! Didn't you see my horns?"

"Guess not." Sky was quiet a few seconds. "Is Joel . . . ?"

"Oh God, no! He's the most hopeless hetero you'll ever meet. It's pathetic."

Well, then, Sky thought to himself, *how do you tell?* Rico met his gaze, and Sky looked down at the salt-shaker.

"Don't worry about it," Rico said.

"I'm not."

They split the tab, and Sky watched an alarming amount of his money disappear into the waiter's apron pocket. Then they were outside in the dark with the wind against them, a last twist of snow cartwheeling overhead. Sky thought about his rubber boots in the hall closet at home.

He felt Rico's cautioning hand on his arm and looked up. Just ahead, Judson Church was a mass of shadows, the snow on its steps glinting under a streetlight. At the curb sat an idling police car. Two officers were thumping on the church's front door.

"They here for you?" Rico whispered.

Sky was already fading back behind a parked car.

Rico turned and sauntered to the church. Sky could just hear his voice, thinned by the wind: "Can I help you, Officers?"

By now Sky was on the other side of the street, head down, walking fast. Of *course* his dad would think of Judson. What made Sky think he'd be safe there?

He reached Sixth Avenue and watched a river of cabs and cars hustling north toward the theater district. His feet felt numb in the wet sneakers. He had a change of socks, but they were inside his briefcase up in the choir loft.

The light turned green, and he crossed. Was he going home after all? If so, he was headed in the wrong direction. There was a bookstore, he remembered, across the street from the Lion's Head. Maybe he could duck in and get warm for a few minutes.

Turning down a familiar block, he found himself passing Olmedo's building.

"Forget it," he said aloud.

He pulled open the heavy door to the entranceway.

"Don't even think about it."

He rang the bell, then stood looking at it as if he'd triggered a bomb.

"Diga!"

Sky opened his mouth but found no words.

"Who the hell is it?" Olmedo's voice crackled over the faulty wires.

"Um," Sky began, but couldn't go on.

There was a long silence.

"Is it you, kid?"

Sky nodded.

The buzzer rang, releasing the lock, and Sky went in.

Sky woke up on the living-room couch to see sunlight streaming in and clumps of snow falling from the branches of an ailanthus tree out in the courtyard. He was safe and unfindable, in the best place in the world. His sneakers and socks, which had spent the night on top of a puffing radiator, were dry.

Olmedo had asked very few questions last night. "Need a place to stay?" he'd said when he opened the door.

Sky began to launch into an explanation, but Olmedo cut him short with a simple "It's okay." He told him where to find a blanket and which piece of furniture to curl up on. So different from Sky's father, who would have conducted an inquisition.

And there were no questions this morning. Demands, yes. That came as a surprise. Olmedo awoke with a coughing fit and called for a glass of water to take his pills with. Then, when it was discovered that the bread was stale and the milk sour, he told Sky to run around to Gristede's and pick up groceries. While he was at it, there was a prescription waiting at Staub's Pharmacy.

Sky didn't know whether to be irritated or honored. He was happy to run errands for this man he admired so much, but he didn't want to be thought of as an errand boy. He had some pride.

"Here, take my keys. Don't lose 'em."

"Okay."

Olmedo made unpleasant sounds as he cleared his throat. "Come right back," he said thickly.

"'Kay."

Irritating, yes, with Olmedo's blind eyes looking past him as if he weren't even there; but Sky's mood brightened as he stepped from the clanking elevator and pushed open the door to the street. It was like a greeting card: GREENWICH VILLAGE IN THE SNOW, the blue mailbox wearing a white hat and the sidewalk snow packed down under the feet of passersby. Striding along, his still-warm sneakers making creaking sounds as he went, Sky allowed himself to fantasize that he lived here, that he was just stepping out to pick up the morning paper.

And that is what he did, plunking down thirty-five cents for the *Village Voice* at the news kiosk. He took it with him into a coffee shop and checked the jazz listings over a cup of really poor coffee and an English muffin with marmalade. There was an article by that guy he'd met last night at the Lion's Head, and sure enough, not a capital letter in the whole thing.

Yes, yes, the errands, he reminded himself, tucking the paper under his arm. Olmedo, he knew, had a standing account at both Gristede's and the drugstore, so Sky wasn't called on to dip into his reserves. He returned with his arms full and humming a cheerful "I Should Care." He tossed the *Voice* on the couch.

"So who's at the Village Gate?" said Olmedo, who was hunched over the keyboard working out a series of dissonant chords.

"Lee Konitz," Sky said before he thought about it. "Wait," he stammered, "how would you . . . ?"

Olmedo modulated into a recognizable key and turned around. "Don't be so impressed. That's the *Village Voice,* right? What would you be reading in it? I'm just sorry you had such lousy coffee."

"Hey, now. There's no *way* you could know that!"

Olmedo waved away Sky's confusion. "Okay, that was a guess. But I live here. I *know* that place on the corner."

"Yeah, but—"

"Kid, you want to be helpful? Brew up a pot for us poor beggars who haven't had any yet."

It took a moment to take this in. "How do you like it?" Sky said.

"Like I like my women. Warm and sweet."

Sky made as little noise as he could because he

wanted to hear Olmedo playing. It was disappointing. Even a master, it seems, practices scales.

Sky came in carrying two coffees. He set one on the piano and sipped at the other, a cracked mug with NEWPORT JAZZ FESTIVAL 1957 on the side.

"Mind if I take a few notes?" Sky said, pulling out his rolled-up composition book.

"Careful, you might copy down my mistakes."

Sky chuckled. "I wouldn't know it was a mistake."

"True." Olmedo clambered up and down the keyboard with a series of chord clusters. "Know why?"

"Why?"

"Because there are no mistakes. You hit a note you didn't mean to hit, you go back and hit it again, harder." He cleared his throat noisily and spat into a wastebasket. "People will say, 'Hey, we thought he was going to hit an F-sharp, but he surprised us. The cat's a genius!'"

"I wish I could make your mistakes."

"You'll make your own."

"They're not as interesting."

Olmedo started a walking bass in the left hand, then rolled into a driving melodic line in the right, no chords at all, just two lines of melody heading in opposite directions, then crossing, colliding, separating. You had a sense of what key he was in, but you wouldn't want to bet on it.

Olmedo stopped in the middle of a phrase and turned around on the bench. "How long you staying, by the way?"

Sky was a little stunned by the question.

"That long, huh?" said Olmedo.

Sky set the mug down. "When, um, do you want me out of here?"

"Yesterday."

"Oh."

There was an extra-long silence.

"I guess we missed that deadline," Olmedo said. "How about tomorrow?"

Tomorrow was Sunday. Sky had no idea what Sunday held for him. "It's your call."

Olmedo looked at him, or seemed to. "You do have a home, am I right?"

"Uh-huh."

"So what has to happen?"

Sky stared down at his cooling coffee. "I don't know."

"Does your daddy have to come and beg?"

The idea was so beyond everything that Sky couldn't respond.

"You don't think he would?"

"I don't think he would, no."

The jazzman nodded. "It's hard for some people. Was for me."

Sky looked up. "You have, um, a son?"

"Had a son."

"What happened?"

Olmedo waved the question away. Sky realized this was a regular gesture with him. "Water under the bridge."

Sky was a little scared to push, but he wanted to know. "Did he run away?"

"He walked away. I'm a horrible person, and he finally had enough of it."

"Did you . . . ?" How do you say this to a man like Olmedo? "Beg?"

A flash of emotion crossed the man's face. "No, I didn't."

"I see."

"So I'm no damn expert on how families are supposed to work. You came to the wrong guy."

Sky looked down.

"Maybe you could let me do some practicing now," Olmedo said.

"You want me to go out?"

"That would be nice."

Sky got up, and Olmedo went back to doing scales, louder and faster than Sky had ever heard scales played. He was still doing them when Sky slipped out and closed the door.

That afternoon Sky went by the church to get his stuff. The side door was unlatched, so he hurried upstairs and found the briefcase in the loft where he'd left it. Sky wanted to stay and run through some tunes, but he was haunted by the fear that a cop might jump out from behind a pew. He continued to feel uneasy until he was out of the building and had turned the corner into another street.

Spotting a phone booth, he pulled open the folding door and slipped in, balancing the briefcase on his knees while he searched for a dime. He dingled it into the slot.

"Yeah," said a familiar voice.

"Max, it's me."

"Hey, where are you?"

Sky briefly told him what was up.

"You *stayed* with the guy?" said Max, impressed. "What's he like?"

Sky couldn't begin to answer that one. "He wants me to leave tomorrow."

"What are you going to do?"

Sky shook his head.

"How's the money holding out?"

That wasn't an easy question either.

"Tell me where to meet you. I can get some money from my mom."

"I don't want your mom's money."

"She won't feel a thing."

"Max, I don't want you stealing from her."

"I'd ask to borrow it, except she's still freaked out about the cops coming over last night."

"Oh no."

"And your dad calling."

"I can't believe this!"

"He accused her of helping to hide you."

"He's an idiot."

"Anyway, she is kind of freaked. I guess your dad is too. He's really looking for you."

"Let him look."

"Right. Tell you what. Can you meet me in an hour at that coffeehouse on Bleecker? Le Figaro? I'll see what I can scrounge."

"Not from your mother."

"I promise."

"And, Max . . ."

"What?"

"If you happen to have Monday's homework assignments, bring them along. I forgot to get them."

"Sky," said Max with a sigh, "you are one weird cat."

An hour is a long time when your feet are freezing. Sky ducked into Le Figaro twenty minutes early, shucking off his sneakers under the table so he could rub his feet. He pulled out his composition book and, after staring awhile at the brass eagles on the espresso machines, began to write. For some reason, ideas came to him. The bridge (or what he called "the middle part") generally led back to a restatement of the theme; but did it have to? Why not cross the bridge into new territory, in a new key? He could always build another bridge to get back.

The brass eagles stared at him. He bent over his book, scribbling in a sort of musical shorthand. When his pencil grew dull, he pulled another from his inside pocket.

Max walked in with Suze Matheson.

"Hey," said Sky, putting his book away.

"Hey," said Suze. She was smiling, but it was a serious smile. No crinkles.

Max slid into a chair. "You okay, man?"

"Sure."

"Turns out Suze is Miss Gotrocks."

She nodded. "I had a little Christmas money saved up. And Jill added another twenty of her own." She took out an envelope and tucked it in his pocket.

"You took a *collection*?"

"Just Jill," said Max. "She's cool. She won't tell anyone."

"She's great," Suze agreed.

"So how is it being a beatnik out here doing the Jack Kerouac *On the Road* thing?" said Max.

Sky looked at him as if he were crazy. "Less fun than you'd think."

"Why not go home?" said Suze.

"Think I should?"

"There are worse things."

He nodded. "I know. But maybe there are better things."

"Like?" Max said.

"You know Rico, at Judson? He ran away when he was sixteen, and he's fine. He's doing just what he wants."

Max and Suze glanced at each other.

"He doesn't have anybody telling him he can't be who he is," Sky went on.

Max nodded. "Of course, he's not as weird as you are."

"Oh, he's plenty weird."

"No, but you're a runaway who wants to keep up with his *homework*."

"And someone," added Suze, "who I *think* wants to go to the dance next Friday."

"God, I forgot!"

"Unless you don't."

"I do! Of course I do."

"Well?" said Max.

The three of them looked at one another.

"We care about you, you idiot," said Suze. She leaned across the little table and gave his shoulder a push.

"You think this is stupid," he said. "You think I should give up and go home."

"I don't know what you should do."

"You think I should just forget about music."

"That's not true!"

Suddenly, Sky was struggling to keep tears out of his eyes. "I don't know what to do," he said hopelessly. "I'm such a mess."

"You're not a mess," said Suze.

Sky shook his head, then fished around for his sneakers.

"You don't have to go," she said.

"No, really," Sky said. He stood up. "Tell Jill thanks for me. You know I'll pay you guys back."

"No hurry," Max said. "Should we meet back here the same time on Monday?"

"Sure."

"Oh, by the way." Max pulled a slim sheaf of looseleaf paper from his pocket. "Here are your freakin' homework assignments."

Sky headed up Thompson toward Washington Square, his briefcase bumping against his leg. Afternoon was beginning to dim, and the kids who'd been playing in the square were straggling off, tossing halfhearted snowballs as they went. The fountain had been drained months ago, and the basin surrounding it was filled with snow and the shadows of snow. Just now a collie was romping through it until his master whistled him back.

Ahead rose the great arch that dominated the north side of the park. It was a beautiful thing, if you didn't look at the graffiti. Sky glanced down a wide walkway and saw a figure sitting on a bench while a crowd of pigeons stepped about in front of him, gurgling and fluttering. Even before he saw the white cane, Sky knew who it was.

He slid onto a bench across from him. "I know you know I'm here," he said.

Olmedo tossed a handful of crumbs, and the pigeons started fussing over them.

"Look," Sky said, "I got a little money today, so if you don't want me staying tonight . . ." His voice trailed away.

Olmedo cleared his throat and spat in the snow. "It's no good," he said to no one in particular.

"What?"

"You give 'em a little and you're stuck. They won't go away."

"But you're not stuck. I told you, I can find a place."

"I'm talking about pigeons."

Sky didn't reply.

"All these damn pigeons, when I'm really interested in that cardinal."

"What cardinal?"

"The one up there on the cross-pipe."

Sky looked up, catching a momentary flash of red

before a bird disappeared into a pipe near the top of the streetlamp. "You're right, he's up there."

"'Course he's up there. You got to feed a lot of pigeons to get one cardinal to come down."

They sat in silence, except when Olmedo hawked up some phlegm and spat in the snow. After a long time a flick of red caught Sky's attention. The cardinal landed at the outer edge of the pigeons and began pecking tentatively.

"He came down!" Sky said.

Olmedo gave a slight smile. "What's he look like?"

"Very pretty. Bright red."

"What's red like?"

"Red, well, it's . . ." Sky was stumped. "It's a warm color. These pigeons are gray, which is a cooler color."

"A warm color," Olmedo repeated.

"It's the color of blood. Fire."

"Yeah, okay."

"Pigeons are the color of ashes."

"That's good."

"He really stands out."

"Fire in the ashes."

Sky found himself shivering. Actually, he'd been shivering for some time.

"You could use some fire yourself," said Olmedo. "You want to help me up?"

Sky gave him a hand, noticing Olmedo wince as he

got to his feet. They were nearly to the edge of the park when the streetlamps suddenly came on.

"Ah," said Olmedo.

Sky was not fooled. "I heard the buzzing too," he said.

"Good boy." They walked on toward Sixth. "I don't know what we have to eat. I think there's some macaroni."

Sky thought a minute. "Why not let me cook up something? How about an omelette with hash browns?"

Olmedo took his arm as they crossed the avenue. "You *cook*?"

"I do most of the cooking at home."

"Man!"

They stopped at the grocer's, and Sky, flush with money, insisted on paying for the onions, potatoes, and other things he would need. He was not a fancy cook, certainly, but he'd seen the box of macaroni in the cupboard and was sure he could do better than that.

They ate well that night. The cheese-and-onion omelette turned out just right, the bacon for once not burned, and the hash browns the way God intended. The place even looked cheerier, since Sky had bought new lightbulbs and replaced the burned-out one in the ceiling. The only depressing moment came when Sky thought about his father, who was hopelessly incompetent in the kitchen. He could imagine him having cornflakes for dinner.

Sky looked at Olmedo across the little table. Actually, he had to look away a few times as Olmedo felt his way around his plate with his fingers. You'd think the guy hadn't had a meal in a month. Pretty soon the two of them were chatting about nothing in particular. That meant music. Sky wanted to know how Olmedo had gotten started on some of his long pieces, like "Regeneration."

"Center of gravity," he replied.

"I don't know what that means."

"Lot of cats play from their head. Some play from their fingers. You can tell right away."

"You mean they're showing off?"

"Yeah. 'Look how fast I can go!'"

"So what do you do?"

Olmedo snorted. "When I'm not a jackass, I play from here." He laid a hand on his skinny belly. "Your gut knows, but you gotta listen to it. Lower your center of gravity."

"Um," Sky began. "Mr. Olmedo . . ."

The old man waited.

"You sure you don't want to show me those last chords of 'Regeneration'?"

"Have you been listening?"

"Yes."

"First of all, I don't know who this 'Mr. Olmedo' is. My name is Art."

"Art." Sky smiled. He'd wanted to call him that for days.

"Second, the chords don't matter. It's how you get to them. If I gave you some chords to copy, you'd be playing them from your fingers."

"Right now I can't play them at all."

"You're not ready to."

Sky looked down. This guy was tough.

"When you play from your gut," Olmedo went on, "you'll come up with your own chords. You'll come up with better chords."

This seemed a good moment to mention that Sky had, in fact, been writing some music of his own.

"So play it," Olmedo said. "Let's hear what you got."

They worked at the piano for a good hour; and by the time Sky got to bed, elated with discoveries, sometime after midnight, he realized that the subject of his leaving had never come up.

Before long Sky began to see that Olmedo's ideas about scales were not so crazy. Sky had always favored certain fingers, limping around the keyboard like a hurt animal on the run. But these new exercises were strengthening his fingers equally. The weak fourth finger in the left hand would never be as nimble as, say, the second in his right, but his control was improving.

Best of all, Olmedo let him practice in the apartment. Sky had told him about the police nosing around the church. Olmedo thought it unlikely that they'd send follow-up search parties, but he didn't argue.

Sunday night, over tuna casserole (another of Sky's concoctions), they talked about the coming week. Sky even brought up the dance.

"I hope you don't want advice," Olmedo said.

"Guess not." Sky poked his noodles around his plate. "I guess I'm supposed to give her a corsage."

"Boy, are you asking the wrong guy!"

"Yeah." He twirled some noodles around his fork. "Is there a flower called a chameleon?"

"Camellia."

"That's it." Sky lapsed into silence. "Oh God, I'll need a tux."

"Don't you have one?"

"At home. I have it for gigs."

"Ah."

"I guess I could sneak home and get it."

Olmedo leaned back, chewing. "You could borrow mine."

"Really?"

"Haven't used it in years. I'm just saving it to be buried in."

They went to the closet and pulled the thing out. It was too big around the shoulders, too short in the sleeves. But Sky liked how flashy it was, the lapels and cummerbund a neon blue satin against the black background, the shirt flamboyantly ruffled.

"I love it!"

"You really need a pink Cadillac to go with it," said Olmedo.

Wow, I'm wearing Art's clothes now, Sky thought. "Mind if I try it on?" In a moment Sky had pulled off his dungarees and stepped into the tuxedo pants.

"Uh-oh," he said.

"Too short?"

"It's not that so much . . ." The pants were short, but the real problem was the whiteness of his legs shining through a dozen tiny holes, like a constellation.

"What is it?"

"Moths."

"Bad?"

"Bad enough."

Olmedo chuckled. "See, if you was dark like me, it wouldn't show."

"Yeah."

"How about I lend you some shoe polish?"

"What do you mean?"

"Just where you show through the holes."

Sky looked at him sideways to see if he was serious. It seemed he was. "We'll see," he said slowly.

With his outfit more or less settled, Sky went back to clear the kitchen table, then sat down with his geometry book. The plan was to give Max his schoolwork tomorrow and pick up the next day's assignments.

He looked around. The apartment could not be called homey—Olmedo had no pictures on the wall or carpets on the floor—but Sky was starting to feel at ease. Although he was afraid to bring it up, the hope was growing in him that he could just stay on. Wasn't he doing his part? Cooking, cleaning up, doing errands, finding stuff when it fell on the floor?

The next afternoon he met Max at Le Figaro, and

they exchanged news. Suze didn't come this time, to
Sky's disappointment. His present life was exhilarating, but it was also lonely.

"Basketball's starting up," Max reported. "Steve
Glass is going to be center again. Oh yes, and Truscott
returned our English papers." Max handed over Sky's
essay with a flourish. It was a B minus. "Should have
been an A," he said.

"You read it?"

"I wanted to see how he'd treat a guy who barged in
on his seduction scene. He gave you as low a grade as
he could get away with."

"He could have flunked me."

Max shook his head. "He might be called on to
defend the grade someday, and he wouldn't be able
to. The way you talk about that play-within-a-play
business is really good."

"Thanks."

"It's unflunkable."

Funny, Sky thought, *how sometimes you can do your best
work out of sheer anger.* They sat and took each other in.

"Am I putting you in a tough position?" Sky said.

"How do you mean?"

"Meeting me like this. They know I'm not in
school, and yet my homework's coming in. You're the
prime suspect."

Max waggled his hand.

"You sure?"

"I can handle those yo-yos."

Sky raised an eyebrow.

"Really," said Max. "It's copacetic."

"If you say so."

"What else?"

"My tuxedo has moth holes in it," Sky said.

"What!"

"Actually, it's Art's tuxedo. He wants me to put some shoe polish on my legs."

Max laughed out loud. "Shoe polish!"

"I'd love it if you had a better idea."

Max thought. "Actually, I might. But I need to talk to Suze. I'll tell you tomorrow."

"How's she doing?" Sky said.

"Da Suze is good. She hasn't quit the magazine yet."

"That's good."

"She's waiting to see how it plays out."

"Truscott will leave her alone if he has any sense."

Max nodded. "Big if."

"Must be creepy, though."

"Yeah."

"Running the meeting with *him* around."

"Actually," Max said, "he hasn't been around much. He showed up at today's meeting and then left."

"Really?"

"He just dropped in to say there wouldn't be any

extra money for the *Review* this year. You know she's been wanting—"

"I know."

"Well, that's all off."

"Did she tell you this?"

"We talk, yeah."

They sat in silence. Sky had the feeling Max wasn't telling him something.

"Everything okay with you?" Sky said.

"Sure, sure."

"Yeah?"

"Everything's copacetic." He pushed his chair back. "Gotta run, though."

"See you here tomorrow?"

"Absolutely." Max winked. "I gotta get your homework, don't I?"

Sky watched him push out the door into the bright, late-afternoon sunlight. Somehow he felt lonelier than before Max had arrived. He reminded himself that he hated his old life, but that didn't help. He missed school, the smell of the classrooms. He missed his old neighborhood, missed dropping in on Mr. Rubin at the deli.

He missed, God help him, his father.

16

Friday came, and Sky found himself in front of the bathroom mirror struggling with an iridescent bow tie.

"How's it coming?" Olmedo called from the living room.

"Terrible."

"Let me see."

The living room was dim, since Olmedo hadn't thought to turn on the light. "How are *you* going to tie it?" Sky said.

Olmedo's hand patted Sky's shoulder and then found the tie. "Like I do everything." In ten seconds it was perfect. "Now get your shoes and get out of here."

The formal shoes were small, but Sky struggled into them and slipped the jacket on.

"You look terrific."

"How would you know?"

"Okay, you look like crap. Just get going."

Sky almost forgot the camellia, which was sitting in a box in the fridge. He wished Olmedo could see how it looked. "Um," he said.

Olmedo stood in the living room, a dark man in a dark turtleneck, his arms folded.

"Thanks," Sky said, "for helping me."

Olmedo probably smiled, but it was hard to tell in the dimness. "Why do I get the idea you need all the help you can get?"

"Yeah. Well, see ya."

"Good luck, kid."

Outside, Sky held his scarf against one ear as he hustled to the subway. He pushed through the turnstile and peered impatiently down the track. The station was not quite deserted. Someone was squatting on a filthy blanket halfway down the platform. It was the guy he'd seen before. So he'd moved over to this station now. Were the air vents warmer? Suddenly, the man turned his eyes on Sky, as if he knew him. Sky turned away.

As the subway roared up through the West Side, Sky tried to calm his nerves. Why should he feel so jumpy? Suze was one of the few people he felt at ease with. The truth (which he would have admitted to no one, even under torture) was that right now he was wearing her tights. That had been Max's brainstorm, to borrow Suze's black dancing tights. They were way too short, of course, and horribly uncomfortable, but the tuxedo looked fine.

So he had no reason to feel nervous. But Suze was

also, tonight, a *date*, and he had never had a real date before. To judge from his reflection in the lobby mirror, he might never have one again. Olmedo's topcoat was at once too big and too small. Sky's hair, grown too long for a crew cut but too short for a regular style, looked geeky despite his efforts to slick it down. And now the damn bow tie had gone crooked. He wrestled with it all the way up in the elevator.

A very large person in an open-necked sport shirt answered the door. Barred the door, you might say. "Yes?"

"Hi, I'm, uh . . ." Sky actually forgot his name. "I'm Alec Schuyler. Is Susan in?"

The person didn't move for a number of seconds. Then, reluctantly, he backed away, like the stone that rolled from the mouth of the cave. There behind him stood an amazing Suze Matheson in a black velvet dress and pearl necklace.

"Hi," she said, her eyes doing that thing they did when she smiled her big smile.

"Hi," he croaked.

"You get her home before one, now."

"Oh, I will, sir."

Susan's mother came out of the kitchen. She was a nice-looking lady, very neat and small boned, dressed in a gray outfit with a flared skirt, as though she were going out to dinner. Sky had the feeling she always dressed that way, even when she sat in the lounger and watched *Perry Mason.*

"You must be Alec," she said, giving his hand an efficient shake.

"Nice to meet you, Mrs. Matheson."

"Oh, Bob, look at that beautiful camellia!"

Suze's father grunted. Sky could tell he didn't give a damn about camellias. He wanted to know about this skinny-necked boy in the crooked bow tie who was going off with his daughter. He kept glancing at Sky while Susan pinned on the flower. Sky didn't feel free of his scrutiny until he was in the elevator and starting down.

"You look . . ." He shook his head.

She glanced at him brightly. "You like?"

"Amazing."

"You're pretty sharp yourself."

That was a lie, but he was grateful for it. Passing the mirror in the lobby, he saw that his slicked-down hair had sprung free again.

Their cab pulled up by the marquee of the Plaza Hotel, and an elderly gent, looking like a guardsman at Buckingham Palace, opened the door with a flourish. If Suze hadn't giggled just then, Sky might have been completely unnerved. Together they swept up the staircase into the dazzling lobby. Sky had been there years ago, when his mother was well enough to take him to lunch; but he'd forgotten how fancy everything was. A violinist was serenading the martini sippers in the Palm Court as Sky and Suze headed to the stairs leading to the ballroom. Miss Dowell, an orchid sprouting from her bosom, directed traffic as people arrived.

Kids who would never look at Sky twice did a double take when they saw who he was with. "Hey, hey, whaddya *say*?" crowed John Wunsch, clapping him on the shoulder.

"Hi, John," Sky answered. "Hi, Rona." Wunsch's date, a tall girl with short bangs and a narrow face, ducked her head and smiled.

A punch on the shoulder almost knocked Sky over. It was Steve Glass, Harmon's star jock, with his arm around buxom Gertrude Somerville. "Missed you in class this week, old man," he said, giving him a wink and a thumbs-up.

Sky was so surprised, he didn't answer. When Steve had moved past, Sky murmured to Suze, "What does a combination of a wink and a thumbs-up mean?"

"It means you are now cool."

"Ah."

"Not as cool as Steve, of course."

"Well, who could be?" Just then Sky spotted Max and signaled, but it took a second to place the girl beside him in the off-the-shoulder, green silk dress.

"Hey, you guys," said this remarkable person, whose voice belonged to Jill Coverton.

They reached the check-in area. Everyone was excited, several girls jumping up and down and screaming at the sight of friends they hadn't seen since three o'clock that afternoon. What struck Sky most was how cordial the teachers were—simply *delighted* to see everyone—as if, for this one night, they were equals. The ancient and much-feared French teacher, known to generations of Harmon students simply as "Mademoiselle," came up and gave Sky a hug.

The ballroom took up two levels, and you came in at the top, where a number of teachers were already seated around linen-draped tables like extras in a costume drama. Then you followed a curving stairway down to the dance floor, surrounded by more tables. These were for the students and their dates. Max led his friends to a spot with a good view. Before long two other couples joined them, kids who'd never been particularly friendly with Sky or Max and who immediately started talking to people at the next table.

"There goes Truscott," muttered Max, nodding toward a table above them.

"Is that his wife with him?" Jill said.

Max nodded. "That's the missus."

They all stared up at the brightly dressed woman with her helmet of perfectly coiffed blond hair. She was sipping a glass of white grape juice, the closest anyone got to having wine.

"She looks nice," said Jill.

"Good figure," said Suze. She looked from one boy to the other. "Well, that's what you're thinking, isn't it?"

"Never crossed my mind," Max said.

A drumroll got everyone's attention as the principal took the mike for his welcoming speech, ending with a mention of every person on the social committee who had worked so hard to make the evening possible.

"Do you think they get along?" said Jill while the principal continued down his list.

"Who?" said Max.

"Mr. and Mrs. Truscott."

He gave his head a tilt. "Why do you ask that?"

She shrugged.

The speech ended, the applause rose and fell, and then waiters came around and set little cups of fruit at everyone's place.

"Well, dig in, gang," said Max.

During the meal kids all over the room began table-hopping to check out their friends. Once the dance music started, it wasn't enough to say something; you had to shout it. For Sky, it was exhausting.

"Dance?" he said as the band launched into an up-tempo "Bye Bye Love."

"Sure!" Suze said.

He led her onto the crowded floor, where he noticed Max and Jill jitterbugging nearby. Jill was a great dancer. After awhile they ended up switching partners, and then the music slowed and Sky found Jill in his arms, smiling against his neck.

"Hey, buster, that's my date," Max called over. "Don't squeeze the merchandise."

"You should talk."

During the band's break they sat at their table sweating and laughing. Sky's legs were itching with heat from the tights, but he didn't mind. The night was all a dream, he knew. It would end, and he'd be out in the street facing the same cold wind and uncertainty as before. For a moment the image of the filthy creature in the subway came to his mind. He forced the vision away.

"Hey, that was a neat essay you wrote for English," he said.

Jill's eyes brightened, her lids lifting. It was like watching a sunrise. "It was great the way you stuck up for me."

"What's the thing with this Coleridge guy?"

"Oh," she said dismissively. "My family's funny. We always read poetry around the kitchen table. One day we got onto 'Kubla Khan,' and I was hooked."

"Sure took Truscott by surprise."

She glanced up at Truscott's table. You could see his wife's bare arm resting on the railing, but he'd disappeared somewhere. "Not the first time," Jill said.

"Oh?"

She shook her head to erase the question. "Not important."

"Tell."

Jill looked around to be sure no one was listening. Max and Suze were deep in their own conversation, and the other two couples had long since left for another table. "Well," she said in an undertone, "last year he tried to put the make on me."

She saw the look on Sky's face. "I'm sure it was just one of those stupid infatuations you hear about, the teacher falling for one of his students. I kind of felt sorry for him."

"What happened?"

"Not as much as he hoped."

Sky looked over at Suze. "Jill," he said slowly, "how would you feel about telling Suze and Max about this?"

Her blue eyes narrowed.

"No, really," Sky said quickly, "there's a reason."

"I haven't told anybody."

"They're not anybody. You can trust them."

"Well . . ."

"Guys," said Sky, touching Suze's wrist, "you need to hear this."

Jill started again, faltering a bit, but soon warmed to the story. Truscott had encouraged Jill's liking for poetry and offered to meet with her now and then after school. She'd felt honored, but during the second meeting she realized he had more than pentameter on his mind.

"First, he wanted me to call him Mark. He said he hoped we'd gotten beyond the foolish conventions between teachers and students."

Sky glanced at Suze. She was looking pale.

"Then he told me I was a special person, someone with a passion—"

"A *passion*?" Suze interrupted.

"That's what he said."

"A passion that nobody but him could understand?"

Jill looked at her strangely. "How did you know?"

Suze's voice turned hard. "And did he stroke your shoulder while he was telling you this?"

"Um . . ." Jill was quiet until her blush subsided. "Actually, it was my knee."

"Your knee."

"Afraid so."

"With me, it was my shoulder."

The girls stared at each other, comprehending more and more.

Max stood up. "Where is this guy?" He scanned the half-empty room. Many of the kids had taken advantage of the band's break to head for the bathrooms.

"Max, sit down," said Suze. "I don't want you getting in trouble."

"He's the one who's in trouble."

"There he is," said Sky.

They all saw him then, sitting at an empty table amid half-consumed Cokes and destroyed desserts. Well, the table was almost empty. He was talking to a girl.

"Looks like he's found someone special," murmured Jill.

"Someone with a hidden passion," Suze said.

"But," said Sky, "his wife's right up there, for godsake!"

Max nodded grimly. "Let's go pay him a visit."

"Are you crazy?" Jill said.

"Max," Suze cautioned.

Max turned to Sky. "You coming?"

"Sure." Sky stood.

"What are you going to *say*?" Jill whispered, getting to her feet.

Suze looked up at them from her seat. "If you think I'm going to be part of this . . ." But then she stood too, and the four of them started across the dance floor to the table where Truscott sat, absorbed in conversation.

He looked up, regarding them mildly. "Having a good time, kids?"

"Great," said Max.

"Do you all know Shannon?" He nodded toward the girl beside him. "She's new."

The girl looked up at them with expressive brown eyes.

"Hi," said Suze and Jill together.

"*Love* that outfit," Jill said, noting the pink satin dress with its suggestion of cleavage.

"Thanks!"

No one knew what to say.

"Well, have fun!" Jill turned to go.

"See you," said Suze.

Sky felt relieved and betrayed. So they weren't going to say anything after all.

They might have left then, except that Max, as an afterthought, said, "Shan, you a writer by any chance?"

"Oh, not yet! Although Mr. Truscott thinks—"

"He thinks you've . . . got talent?" Max suggested.

Suze visibly flinched.

"Well . . ." Shannon colored. "Mr. Truscott's been helping me—"

"Still 'Mr. Truscott'?" said Suze suddenly, her voice shaky. "Isn't he on a first-name basis with you yet?"

Truscott looked up sharply.

Sky found it hard to breathe. He could see that Suze was as scared as he was, but she was *doing* it. She was saying the words.

"He hates all those foolish conventions," Suze went on, her cheeks flushed. "Don't you, *Mark*?"

"Susan, I don't know what you're trying to do—"

Sky's heart was beating hard, but he spoke up: "I think," he said, "she's blowing the whistle on you."

"For heaven's sake!" Truscott burst out, pushing his chair back and standing. "If you must bring up old misunderstandings, let's talk about them somewhere else. Not during the school dance!"

The four of them—five, with Shannon—went dead silent. Arguing with an angry teacher was beyond them. Even Max faltered.

Sky heard a male throat clearing loudly. "Could somebody tell me what's going on?" It was John Crowder, the principal. He was a nebbishy sort, with blinking, pale blue eyes and thinning hair, but Sky was glad to see him.

That didn't mean he could speak. "Um," he began.

The kids looked at one another.

"It's nothing, John," Truscott said with an easy smile. "A grade thing, that's all."

"Grades?"

"That's it."

Crowder nodded. "Well, this is hardly the time or the place."

"Exactly what I said."

Sky felt himself choking. So often, in Truscott's

class, he'd found himself voiceless. It was happening again.

"Please," Crowder said, looking at the students, "don't bother your teacher with this tonight."

No one said anything.

"Now go back and enjoy yourselves, everyone. That's what I intend to do." The principal nodded and turned away.

"He's touching his students!" The words flew out of Sky's mouth.

Slowly, Crowder turned back. "Could you repeat that?"

At first Sky couldn't. But the second time was a little easier. "He's . . . he's touching his students."

Everyone was silent.

Crowder stared at Sky; then he took in the others around the table. "This is a very serious accusation, Mr. Schuyler."

Again, no one spoke.

"Who is saying this?"

"I'm saying it," said Suze Matheson.

"Now, hold on!" Truscott cut in.

"And I'm saying it," said Jill Coverton.

Crowder's forehead was high enough to form several frowns, and he brought them all into play. "I think we should talk about this on Monday, in my office."

"I'm afraid we're already talking about it," said Suze.

"Well, you should stop."

"That's what I was telling them," said Truscott.

"Right now," Crowder finished.

Stop they did, beginning a fading retreat to their own table. Sky noticed that Shannon had stood up now and was making a retreat herself.

Crowder went up to Sky. "Monday morning, before first period," he said quietly.

"Yes, sir."

"That means all of you."

"Yes, sir."

"Thank you, Mr. Crowder," said Jill, giving him a good smile.

The dancing began again, but the four friends didn't stay long. Whispered word had spread quickly, and people started sidling up and asking if what they'd heard was true. They had heard any number of things.

Jill said, "How about we get out of here?"

"Check," said Max.

Sky helped Suze on with her coat, careful not to crush the corsage. He was feeling overheated, and it was a relief to step outside into the surprise of falling snow. Big flakes fluttered down, covering the nymph in the Plaza fountain and slowing traffic to a moan.

Soon snowballs were flying. Suze squealed as a lucky throw sent snow down the neck of her coat.

"Hey," said Jill, nodding toward the lights of the Mayflower coffee shop across the street. "Anybody want something to eat?"

By the time they got through the deep snow at the curb and made it to the other side, their shoes were a mess; but it all seemed very funny. There was something fine about barging into a fluorescent-lit coffee shop, being dressed in tuxedos and all the rest, and sitting at the counter sipping ice-cream sodas and drinking coffee.

Briefly, the talk turned to Mrs. Truscott.

"She knows what he does," Jill said definitely. "I bet she's always known it."

"Really? You think so?" Suze said.

Sky was only half listening. He was thinking of another coffee shop, a week ago, after he'd been riding on subways all night. Remembering the look of the abandoned Ford showroom at five in the morning and how hungry he'd felt, he suddenly looked up and signaled to the waiter.

"I'd like a side order of bacon, please."

"Just bacon?"

"That's it." He looked around at his friends. "Anybody else want some bacon?"

"I'll have some," Max said.

The girls shook their heads.

"Two orders. Crisp, please."

"Bacon and ice cream." Jill shook her head. "What a combo."

"Sky, you sure you're not pregnant?" said Suze, and they were all laughing again.

Cabs aren't easy to come by in a snowstorm, but Max finally flagged one down, a clunky old Yellow cab with a heater that blew hot air in your face. Sky perched on a little fold-down seat while Max sat behind him surrounded by girls.

"Hey," said Sky, "how come he rates?"

"Come on back," said Jill.

So he did, turning the ride into a tangle of knees and smart-mouth remarks. Sky and Suze got out first, since he had promised to get her home by one. At the door Suze held Sky's cheeks with her two cold hands and planted a worm-cold kiss on his forehead.

"You were wonderful tonight, Mr. Schuyler."

"You too."

They looked at each other.

"You want your tights back?" he said.

"Do you mind?" She was laughing.

"Sure." He made as if to undo his belt.

"Like you really would."

"You don't think I would?"

"Wait, let me get my dad. We can all watch."

Sky glanced at the door latch. "On second thought," he said.

She gave him a considering look. "You going to see Jill again?"

"Jill?"

"Jill Coverton. She goes to our school. She likes you."

"You don't?"

She punched his arm. "No, I hate you. But I mean, she *likes* you."

"Really?"

"Think about it."

He nodded. He would have liked to have a passionate good-night kiss from Susan Matheson just then, but he knew she was right. Probably, they would always be arm-punching friends. "Well," he said, "see ya."

"Thanks, Sky. It was the best time."

The snow was thinning a bit and the wind picking up as he made his way to the subway station and pulled out his fifteen cents for a token. The cement was wet from snowmelt, and by the time the subway came, Sky's feet were numb. In his pocket his fingers touched the two keys to Olmedo's place. Would the old guy be up waiting for him? He was hard to figure. Sometimes he could be so brusque; at other times he was almost fatherly, like lending Sky this wacky tuxedo.

At Sheridan Square, Sky climbed the stairs to the street. Thinking of Olmedo made him think of jazz, and pretty soon he was humming "I Should Care."

It'll be good to get out of these shoes, he thought.

That was the last thought he had before he heard the whoosh of a police car passing him, its red light twirling wildly. It skidded to the curb in front of Olmedo's building, and the doors burst open on both sides. From the driver's side, a policeman emerged. From the other, struggling a little, came a stocky man with a bald head.

"*Alec!*" the man called. "Alec! Thank God!"

17

Sky didn't know what his father was expecting as he stood with his hand on Sky's shoulder in the dark hallway, but he guessed it was not the elderly black man with the bulbous forehead who opened the door, directing milky eyes at a corner of the ceiling and saying, "I see you got company."

The cop flopped open his wallet to show his badge, not that Olmedo was looking. "Ben Florid, New York Police. Are you Arturo Olmedo?"

"Last I heard."

"Mind if I ask a few questions?"

"Inside. I got nosy neighbors."

"I'm sorry, Art," said Sky.

"No, no, this had to happen," he said, tying closed his stained bathrobe. He held out his hand to Quinn. "You must be Sky's father."

Quinn did not shake it, but walked past into the living room.

"Dad!" said Sky, appalled. "This is Art Olmedo. I know you don't know who he is, but he's a famous musician."

"I don't care if he's Albert Schweitzer."

"Mind if I sit down?" Olmedo shuffled over to his chair, wincing as he lowered himself into it.

Quinn folded his arms across his chest and paced while the cop asked questions.

"We're not charging you with anything, Mr. Olmedo. But you know, Mr. Schuyler has been looking for his son for the last week. Has he been staying with you the whole time?"

Olmedo looked around at the one silent spot in the room. "How long has it been, kid?"

"About a week, I guess." Sky went and clicked on the little lamp by the piano. Then he shucked off his topcoat and sat on the couch, his blue lapels faintly gleaming.

"And how," Florid continued, "did Alec happen to end up staying here with you?"

The jazzman cleared his throat noisily. "He rang my doorbell."

The officer was writing this down.

Quinn burst out: "And you just let him stay here, a perfect stranger, no questions asked?"

"We're friends," Olmedo answered.

"Friends with my son?"

"He likes jazz. I like jazz."

Sky kept his amazement to himself, as if it were no

big deal that Olmedo had just called him his friend.

"Also, he saved my hide. I was crossing a street, and a car clipped me. He got me home."

"*Alec* did that?"

"Is that enough reason to let him stay?"

Officer Florid gave his pants a hitch. "Sounds like a reason to me. So look. Everybody all right here? Don't need me anymore?"

"We're hunky-dory," said Quinn.

"Nice to meet you, Mr. Olmedo. Mr. Schuyler, you have my card."

Quinn nodded. He and Sky watched the cop leave while Olmedo stared straight ahead as before.

"What now?" said Sky, remembering suddenly all the reasons he didn't like his father.

"Let's get out of here," Quinn said.

"You going to drag me home?"

Quinn flashed a look at his son, but he held his temper. "Don't you want to come home?"

"Why would I?"

Again, his father held back. This was new for him, this holding back. "I've been worried about you."

"I'm fine."

Quinn sat on the piano bench and faced him. "You *look* fine. Where'd you get the outfit?"

"Art lent it to me."

Quinn nodded again. "How was the dance?"

"Good," he said warily. "How'd you know about that?"

"I've known about it for a while."

"You have?"

"Let's say I didn't think it would improve our relationship if I had the cops show up at the Plaza Hotel."

Sky took this in. "Did you also know where I was staying?"

"Since Wednesday." Quinn ran his hand over the dome of his head. "I needed time to find out who this character was you were staying with."

Sky glanced at Olmedo, who continued staring straight ahead.

"Today I found out. That's why I had to step in."

"What are you talking about?"

"Do you know he's a drug addict?"

"What!"

"It's all there in the police reports."

"They're lying!"

"Am I lying, Mr. Olmedo?" said Quinn, giving the man a look.

The jazzman didn't reply.

"What would you do, Alec, if you found out somebody you cared about was living in a slum with a drug addict?"

"First of all, this is hardly—"

"Did you know he had a son?" Quinn interrupted.

Sky glanced over at Olmedo. "I knew that."

"And did you know he turned his own son on to drugs?"

"You're crazy!"

"Ask him."

"I don't need to ask him!"

"Then I will. Accurate so far, Mr. Olmedo?"

Olmedo looked up, his sightless eyes scanning the wall. "It's funny," he said, "how you can be right and wrong at the same time."

"You deny being a drug addict?"

"Don't bother answering him," said Sky with disgust.

"Of course I'm an addict. I'll always be an addict. I'm just not a *practicing* addict."

"And you had a son who died of a heroin overdose."

Olmedo's eyes wandered randomly.

"True or not?"

"You have no idea what you're saying."

"A simple enough question."

"Leave him alone!" Sky burst out. "Why are you interrogating him?"

"Because I love you!" Quinn shot back.

The room was silent.

Olmedo nodded. "That's the first smart thing you said tonight."

Sky muttered, "You have a damn funny way of showing it."

Olmedo raised his head. "I will answer your question, Mr. Schuyler. I did not turn my son on to heroin. I just couldn't turn him *off* of it."

"But you were an addict yourself."

"Dad!"

"That's when I stopped. Nothing will get you off drugs faster than finding out what it does . . . to someone . . ." His voice broke off.

Quinn seemed struck by this. He nodded soberly. "All right."

"You have no idea."

"I believe you."

"Did you check the dates on those reports?" Olmedo said.

"Not really."

"The last one was eleven years ago."

Quinn rubbed his hand over his chin.

"I been clean since."

Sky glanced from one to the other. The two could not be more different; and yet, for this moment, they seemed to connect.

"All right," Quinn said at last. He clapped his hands on his knees and got up. "I'm glad you told me this," he said. "It makes me feel better."

"You're welcome. It makes me feel worse."

"I suppose it would." He looked over at Sky. "Well, son, shall we go?"

Sky glanced up. "I'm staying here."

"What! Why?"

"You wouldn't understand."

"What wouldn't I understand?"

Sky shook his head. "That this so-called drug addict has been more of a father to me—"

"Kid," said Olmedo softly, "don't."

"Well, it's true!"

"He's your father. I'm just . . . an intermission."

"Alec," Quinn interrupted. "Look, I know I've been a little rough on you."

"I don't *care* if you're rough on me!" Sky snapped.

"Then what are you talking about?"

"You have to understand what it means when I tell you what I want to do with my life and you tell me to go to hell."

"I never said—"

"You have to understand when you throw out the piano—"

"I didn't throw out—"

"Sold it. Whatever you did."

"I didn't exactly sell it."

"Whatever you did."

"I put it in storage."

"What?"

"I put it in storage. I wanted to teach you a lesson. It was stupid, all right?"

Sky didn't know what to say.

"Listen to your father," said Olmedo.

"It's too late," Sky said.

"What do you mean, 'too late'?" Quinn's face was getting red. "I'm telling you we still have the piano. It's sitting in the goddam living room!"

"Thanks. I don't want it."

"Son, I'm not going to beg."

"Oh, I know that!"

"I'm warning you. I'll walk right out of here!"

"Go ahead. Why'd you come in the first place?"

"I had this crazy idea I wanted my son back home!"

"I *am* home."

"You call this home?"

The words hung in the air several seconds.

"Dad," Sky said quietly, "why don't you just go?"

Quinn looked stunned. He began struggling with the buttons on his coat. His fingers were clumsy, and two of the buttons came undone again. Finally, he gave up. "Alec," he said. "Don't."

"Don't what? I'm not doing anything."

"Come home."

"Dad, I don't think so."

"You don't know what this week's been like."

So, thought Sky, quietly amazed, *he's begging after all.* "What's it been like?"

"Lousy."

Olmedo, who hadn't said a word, locked his hands behind his head and leaned back.

"I don't know," said Sky. "You're too sure of what's good for me."

Quinn threw up his hands. "Okay. I'm not perfect, in case you didn't notice."

Sky didn't argue with that.

Olmedo leaned forward into their conversation. "Try it."

Sky looked down at his wet shoes. This was an interesting situation. "You think I should?"

"I think you should, yeah."

Sky looked at his shoes some more. "All right," he said.

Quinn slapped his leg.

"Good," said Olmedo, "because I was going to kick you out anyway."

"What?"

"You got a home. You should go to it."

Sky looked hard at his sightless face. "There's something else, isn't there?"

"No."

"You taught me how to listen, remember?"

Olmedo didn't answer.

"Well, I'm listening. I think there's something else."

"I'm telling you, there's nothing. . . . Okay, it's your cooking. I hate your damn cooking."

"Art . . ."

"Okay, okay." Olmedo took a breath. "I'm going into St. Vincent's next week for some tests."

Sky closed his eyes.

"No big deal, but I don't want you rattling around here by yourself."

"I don't like this."

"I'm not crazy about it myself."

"Can I come and see you? When will you be out?"

"Soon."

"I don't like this," he said again.

Olmedo waved the words away. "Take care of your boy, Mr. Schuyler."

"I surely will." Quinn crossed the room to shake his hand.

"And now, if you don't mind . . ." Olmedo had begun rubbing his forehead with his fingertips.

"You all right?" said Sky.

"I'm beautiful. A little bushed, maybe."

"We'll go." Sky went into the kitchen and drew a glass of water. "Here, take your pills." He waited while Art swallowed them.

"Tux work out okay?" Olmedo said.

"It was the hit of the evening."

"I bet. Mind hanging it up for me?"

Sky changed into his old clothes and looked around under the couch for his socks. He jingled the apartment keys. "You want these back?"

Olmedo hesitated. "Better hang on to them." He struggled to his feet and went to the bedroom door. "I think you can move on to Coltrane now," he said to the wall. "Next time sing me the solo from 'Giant Steps.'"

"Alec *sings?*" said Quinn incredulously.

"Oh, yes, he sings."

"I never heard him sing."

"It's not pretty."

"I can't believe he sings for you!"

"Mr. Schuyler," said Olmedo, "your son is full of surprises."

Quinn shook his head.

"Well," said Olmedo, looking nowhere in particular, "so long, kid."

Sky didn't answer.

"Get your coat," said Quinn.

Sky didn't move. He stood between the two men. He was definitely not going to cry. Slowly, he slipped on the coat and zipped it, then hoisted the briefcase. "You're not through with me, you know," he said.

"Oh, I know that," Olmedo said.

Quinn shepherded Sky out the door and pulled it

shut with a bang. "Some elevator," he said, pushing the button.

They waited, listening to the wind in the shaft.

"Wait! I forgot something!" Sky pulled out his keys.

"Leave it."

"No, hold the elevator a minute."

Letting himself in, he found Olmedo where he'd left him, leaning against the door of the bedroom. "I forgot my composition book."

"Ah."

There it was, on top of the piano. Sky tucked it in his briefcase. He paused. Then, before he thought about it, he went up and grabbed Olmedo and held him hard. The old man didn't hug him back, but he didn't push him away, either. Finally, he raised a skinny hand and set it gently on top of Sky's head.

"It's okay," Olmedo said.

"I don't like this," said Sky, his eyes hot.

"I know."

"I hate it."

"Yeah," Olmedo said quietly. "I hate it too."

18

"For godsake, Alec, can you hold it *down?*" His father was calling from the top floor, his round head peering over the banister. Sky couldn't blame him. He'd spent almost an hour this bright Saturday morning working on the second section of "Circle of Rain." That had to be tough to put up with.

Yes, the piece had sections. You might almost say "movements." In the last couple of months it had evolved well beyond the usual A-B-A form into a fourteen-minute . . . something or other. Not all of it was written out, of course—there were spaces left open for three improvised solos of sixteen bars each—but it was still a formidable hunk of composing.

"All right," he said. "I'm just . . ." He made another jab, then another, but the chord he was looking for eluded him. Olmedo could've helped with this, but he was back in the hospital.

"Alec, I'm serious. I can't think."

"Okay, okay!" Funny. Sky didn't have any trouble making himself heard these days. Maybe it was all that singing he'd been doing.

A breeze flew through the open window and flapped the pages of his composition book. He knew he was pushing the season: April wasn't far enough along to be warm, but the air kept him alert. He had no time for hazy thinking. Since moving back home a little over three months ago, he felt perpetually in a hurry. It didn't have to do with his homework load or his meager social life. It was Olmedo, in and out of the hospital, one piece of bad news after another. And his father with those damn heart pills. Not to mention his mother, dead at forty-six. There were time limits. Sky had work to do and no time to lose.

He ignored the first three rings of the phone, then snatched it up.

"Hey, guy," said Max.

"Hey."

"You gotta save me. I'm memorizing 'The Charge of the Light Brigade.'"

"I'm sorry."

"Yeah. Miss Buffin is such a . . ."

"Drone?" Sky offered.

"Almost makes you miss Truscott."

"Yeah, well . . ."

"Recovered from the assembly yet?"

"I've forgotten about it."

It was almost true. Last week's long-delayed and finally rescheduled assembly had turned into a scandal;

but "in the greater scheme of things"—one of his mother's big expressions—it didn't matter very much. Certain things mattered. Sky's music mattered. His friends mattered. The sensibilities of timid school administrators mattered not in the least.

It had been a surprise that the assembly happened at all. It wasn't the same event that his father had vetoed last October, but it was close enough that Miss Dowell had to call Quinn up and ask his permission all over again. This time Quinn gave the okay. He was more easygoing these days with Sky. At least he was trying.

"I don't think old man Crowder's going to forget about it for a long time," said Max.

"What did he expect?"

"We called it a music and poetry assembly, so he probably figured Alfred Lord Tennyson was going to show."

"Or Coleridge."

"Anybody but Corso."

Sky thought about Suze, how gleeful she'd been the day before the event. Gregory Corso had finally returned her calls, and she'd gotten him to say he'd come, although Ginsberg could not. "Gregory grooves on me," Suze had explained with a giggle.

"He what?"

"Do you think I'm groovy?"

"Um, sure."

"Well, I'm here to tell you, I am one groovy chick."

But when the day came, there wasn't a beatnik to be seen. Sky, Max, and Rico (brought up specially from Judson to play bass) stalled for time, tossing off a couple of jazz riffs to polite applause. Still no poet. Max pulled out his copy of Corso's *Gasoline*, trying to figure how he could read the poems while playing drums. Jill offered to help, but then Suze walked in, escorting a smiling, confused-looking Corso, his hair tousled, as if he'd just climbed out of bed.

In faded blue jeans and a longshoreman's cap, he looked wildly foreign among all the ties and sports jackets and neatly creased khakis, but he seemed amused by it, his eyes lively and disobedient. He looked out over the crowd and said how totally insane it was to be here and how Sky and his musician friends were the living end. Then Rico laid down a quietly thumping bass line, and Corso got started. He sparked some laughter with "The Mad Yak." But then he went into a long (a *lonnngg*) thing called "Bomb," a surrealistic tirade of antiwar imagery, and pretty soon the audience was squirming. Sky was busy with runs and chord clusters, but a quick glance up showed him the frozen face of the principal as the poem crescendoed, Corso's voice rising to a triumphant shout:

". . . nights ye BOOM   ye days ye BOOM
BOOM BOOM ye winds   ye clouds ye rains
go BANG ye lakes   ye oceans BING . . . !"

Max was having such a great time on the cymbals, he didn't notice the ancient French teacher, her face stricken, being led out by Miss Dowell. When the poem crashed to a close, the room fell silent. Finally, the geometry teacher, Mr. Johanssen, clapped his heavy hands together, and others joined in. The hall cleared quickly, and Sky, Max, and Suze found themselves in the principal's office. Sky couldn't be bothered defending himself. A week later he barely remembered the event.

"We getting together later for a practice at Judson?" Max said.

"Good. Mind if I stop at the hospital on the way?"

"Done."

Sky was always alone when he went to visit Olmedo, but today he arrived at St. Vincent's to find Suze talking with Max outside the entrance. The day had grown warmer, and Suze's blue turtleneck showed through her unbuttoned coat.

"Mind if I tag along?" she said. "I'd kind of like to meet this guy."

"He won't be speaking, you know," Sky said, gesturing to his throat.

"I heard."

"As long as you don't expect anything."

Reaching the oncology wing, Sky led his friends down several corridors and stopped by a room with a half-open door.

"Art," he said. "You awake?" He poked his head in.

Sky was struck at how diminished Olmedo looked since just a few days ago, his head a fistful of dark bones on a white pillow. Clear liquid of some kind was dripping from a plastic bag into his arm. He turned in Sky's direction and raised a hand, palm up.

"He wants me to introduce you guys," Sky said. "Art, these are my friends, Max Rosen and Suze Matheson. Max plays drums. Suze is our business manager."

"Hello, Mr. Olmedo," said Suze, her voice warming the room.

"Hi," said Max, jumping in after her. "This is a real pleasure!" He held out his hand, but then realized that wasn't going to work. He ended up putting it in his pocket.

Olmedo nodded. He pointed a thumb toward Max, then redirected it to the ceiling, raising his eyebrows slightly.

"Yeah," Sky said, "he's good. Of course, he'd be better if he studied with you."

Olmedo compressed the left side of his mouth

slightly, dismissing Sky's remark. Then he made a fist and poked the thumb toward his mouth.

Sky looked around and saw the pitcher on the side table. "Water?"

Olmedo nodded. Sky poured a plastic cupful and handed it to him, and they all watched him drink it. What do you do when the guy you've come to visit can't see or talk?

"I mainly wanted to thank you, Mr. Olmedo," said Suze, "for helping Sky out last winter."

He frowned.

"I don't know what would have happened if you hadn't been there."

Though his eyes weren't directed at them, the jazzman managed to point his thumbs pretty accurately at Suze and Sky. He brought his two hands together and made dancing motions, then raised an eyebrow.

"That's ancient history," said Sky.

"What?" said Max, totally confused.

Sky looked at Art. "You're asking about the dance, right?"

He nodded.

"I think he wants your version, Suze. He's heard mine."

"Well," said Suze, smiling broadly, "I can tell you that your friend is a wonderful dancer."

Eyebrow.

"You should have seen him flashing around the dance floor in that tuxedo."

"Untrue," Max interrupted. "I had to rescue you several times so you wouldn't get trampled."

Both eyebrows.

"Max, stop, you're ruining my story."

"Let's just say he's better on his fingers than on his toes."

Olmedo took this in silently.

"He's really getting pretty decent on the piano," Max went on.

Olmedo wiggled his hand in the air, meaning, *So-so.*

He then put a finger on Sky's wrist to get his attention. He cupped a hand to the side of his mouth and pointed to Sky's chest.

"Guys," said Sky, "I think Art wants to tell me something privately. Is that right, Art?"

The old man nodded.

"Oh, okay!" said Max brightly.

"I'll be out in a minute," Sky said.

Suze took the old man's hand in both of hers. "Thanks again. You did a good thing."

He let her have a trace of a smile.

"*Great* to meet you, sir," said Max. He gave Sky a high sign and went out with Suze.

Olmedo turned to Sky. He pressed his thumb and

forefinger together and turned his hand back and forth a couple of times.

"Okay," said the boy.

Art held out two brown index fingers and made little circles with them.

"Tape?"

Olmedo nodded.

"Where'd you leave it?"

Two dark hands played a chord in the air.

"Okay. You want me to bring it here?"

Olmedo shook his head. He took Sky's wrist again, meaning, *Listen to me, you idiot.* Then he poked the boy in the ribs.

"What?"

Olmedo poked him again.

"You want me to have it?"

Olmedo leaned his head back and nodded.

"Really?"

Olmedo didn't respond. He was not a person to repeat himself.

"Thanks."

Olmedo closed his eyes. Sky recognized it as his new way of saying, *And now, kid, if you don't mind . . .*

"Art?"

No response.

"You're the best."

Olmedo's eyes remained closed, but he reached a

skinny hand over and patted Sky lightly on the arm. That was also a new way of saying something. Something that now he would never put into words.

Max looked up when Sky stepped out in the hall.

"He wants me to pick up something. Why don't I meet you guys down at Judson?"

"Done and done."

In the elevator Suze turned to Sky. "It's amazing how you knew what he was saying."

"Yeah," Max said, "it's like the two of you had a special language."

"I was just listening, that's all."

"Yeah, well, I was listening and I didn't hear a thing."

"Won't he ever be able to speak again?" said Suze.

Sky hesitated. "They went after the cancer in his throat. There wasn't much left of his voice box when they got through."

"It's too horrible."

Sky nodded. Horrible indeed. *Especially,* he thought, *since they didn't get it all.* But he couldn't bring himself to say that.

They pushed open the glass doors and walked out into the April sunlight.

"Well," said Sky.

"Well," said Max.

Suze went on tiptoe to plant a kiss on Sky's forehead.

Then she and Max headed off down the block, a twirl of spring wind blowing a newspaper after them. Sky watched for a while. Friends.

But now he was noticing how they walked together, closer than necessary. As they neared the end of the block Max took Suze's hand. She leaned her head against his shoulder.

Sky felt as if he'd been struck in the chest. *You knew this,* he said to himself, trying to explain away the feeling. *You had to have known they were a couple.*

At the dance were they?

Yes, he realized, remembering whispered conversations.

Then why didn't they just go to the dance together?

Obvious. (And here Sky felt a second blow.) *Her father. Her anti-Semitic father.*

And what does that make you?

(Blow three.) *It makes you an idiot.*

Sky walked south, not watching the streets. Somehow he ended up at Sheridan Square, and then he found himself on Washington Place.

It's not really a betrayal, he told himself.

Oh?

He pulled open the door to Olmedo's building, checked the mailbox, and stood waiting for the elevator. For five whole minutes he hated Max Rosen. How he felt about Suze he couldn't have said.

He was scarcely aware of the elevator ride to the sixth floor or of his letting himself into the apartment.

Max the traitor.

He remembered that time meeting him at Le Figaro and thinking there was something Max wasn't telling him. Well, mystery solved.

He stared across the empty room and out the window at the ailanthus tree with its tight, unfurling leaves. He was here for something. *Oh, yes.* He went to the piano. There stood a thin cardboard box with the word *Sky* scrawled unevenly across the top. Inside was a reel of tape.

Olmedo had never given him a present before.

He sat on the piano bench and reached over to the side table where the tape recorder sat, a heavy gray machine the size of a suitcase. He wound the end of the tape around an empty spool and pushed PLAY.

The speakers let out a soft hissing sound, and then Olmedo's voice came on. He sounded hoarse, but there he was, speaking! Tears started in Sky's eyes even before he understood the words.

"Testing," said the voice. "Tomorrow's the operation, so I'm laying down this track today, in case. I call it 'Fire in the Ashes.'" He paused to clear his throat loudly. "It's for a friend of mine, name of Sky, who taught me the color red. Hope you like it, kid."

The voice was replaced by an electronic hum. That

stopped after a few seconds, and the piano began, soft and slow, A minor to E minor and back to A minor, a simple, home-fried blues.

Sky wiped his eyes.

The piece never speeded up, but it grew steadily more complex, a simple tuber of sound sending out hair-thin roots till you were looking at those simple chords through a filigree of thirty-second notes. With the pattern established, Olmedo threw in some high single notes in a different key, an injection of a foreign voice over the tumult below. Sky recognized it at once as the intervals of the cardinal's song. The effect was sensational.

The piece built and curled around itself for several minutes before resolving into a wholly unforeseeable F major. And that was it, except for a faint hissing as the empty tape ran through.

Sky sat listening to the emptiness. "Art," he murmured. "For godsake, Art, don't die."

With the tape reel tucked in his windbreaker and fists in his pockets, Sky strode down West Fourth Street, eyes to the sidewalk. His mind was a tangle, and he didn't even try to sort out the strands—the music he'd heard, his anger at Max, the swing of birds overhead, and for some reason, Jill Coverton's eyes as they lifted toward him. Yes, those slow-lidded eyes, a surprised blue. It was as though he was free to think about them now.

But why now? Hadn't he known for months that Suze was not girlfriend material? Surely it hadn't taken seeing her with Max to teach him that!

No, he thought, *but it's one thing to know something; it's another thing to realize it.*

A convoy of pigeons sailed over the turret of Judson Church. He stood before the door and suddenly knew he wasn't going in. He wasn't ready to be all chummy with Max and Suze. Maybe tomorrow.

Instead, he crossed the street into Washington Square and found himself in the walkway where Olmedo always sat when he came to feed the birds. Sky took the bench opposite Olmedo's. The afternoon had turned beautiful, a warming breeze cuffing his hair.

Yes, he was angry, but he might as well face who he was angry at. Not Max. Not really. He looked up at the tops of the budding elms. *"Enough damn dying, all right?"* he shouted. At the far end of the walkway a woman with a pram turned to glance at him, then hurried on. He couldn't blame her. He felt sort of shocked himself.

"No more Edsels!"

Hey, he thought, *this is kind of fun. Why have you never shouted before?*

"No more Truscott Christmas trees!"

Two kids over by the fountain stopped tossing a ball to look at him.

This is what crazy people sound like, he thought. *You'd better cool it.* Sky leaned back, letting the breeze wash over him. He laid his arms along the back of the bench and stretched out his legs, crossing them at the ankles. That reminded him of something, and he shouted suddenly: *"'Christ climbed down from His bare Tree this year'!"*

Now, that felt good!

It was time to come down from his own bare tree. Trees were for the birds. *Yes,* he thought, *trees, and the cross-pipes of lampposts.*

And for the next hour, with his eyes closed and a smile playing about his lips, Sky watched all the birds in sight.

ACKNOWLEDGMENTS

I am grateful to my brother, Odin Richard Townley, for memories of life under the Third Avenue El; to John Weisman for reminding me about our Greenwich Village haunts; and to Paula Grossman for a story about matzoh balls. My deep thanks, as well, to my agent, Amy Berkower, and my editor, Richard Jackson.